Mills & Boon
Best Seller Romance

*Books you will enjoy
by VIOLET WINSPEAR*

BRIDE'S DILEMMA

Tina married John Trecarrel in haste—and had time to repent when she found that she had to compete with the memory of his beautiful first wife and that he was attracted to Joanna's equally beautiful cousin Paula.

A GIRL POSSESSED

Janie was an actress—but was she a good enough actress to pretend to be married to Pagan Pentrevah, to keep his ex-wife Roxanne at bay? More to the point, was she actress enough to conceal her own hopeless love for Pagan?

LOVE IS THE HONEY

At eighteen, having spent all her life in a convent, Iris agreed with the Mother Superior that it was time she ventured into the world to see what life was like. So she took a job as governess to the small son of the overwhelming Zonar Mavrakis—and found out with a vengeance!

PALACE OF THE POMEGRANATE

Life had not been an easy ride for Grace Wilde and she had every reason to be distrustful of men. Then, in the Persian desert, she fell into the hands of another man, Kharim Khan, who was different from any other man she had met ...

CHILD OF JUDAS

BY
VIOLET WINSPEAR

MILLS & BOON LIMITED
LONDON · TORONTO

All the characters in this book have no existence outside the imagination of the Author, and have no relation whatsoever to anyone bearing the same name or names. They are not even distantly inspired by any individual known or unknown to the Author, and all the incidents are pure invention.

The text of this publication or any part thereof may not be reproduced or transmitted in any form or by any means, electronic or mechanical, including photocopying, recording, storage in an information retrieval system, or otherwise, without the written permission of the publisher.

This book is sold subject to the condition that it shall not, by way of trade or otherwise, be lent, resold, hired out or otherwise circulated without the prior consent of the publisher in any form of binding or cover other than that in which it is published and without a similar condition including this condition being imposed on the subsequent purchaser.

First published 1976
Australian copyright 1981
Philippine copyright 1981
This edition 1981

© Violet Winspear 1976

ISBN 0 263 73497 8

Reproduced, printed and bound in Great Britain by Cox & Wyman Ltd, Reading

CHAPTER ONE

'WHAT devil's game do you think you are playing?'

Fenny stood there in Penela's going-away suit and only the soft grey shoes were a size too large, so she had needed to cut inners from the lid of the shoe box. What could she say? What defence had she to offer in the face of the unforgivable thing she had done?

But Penela had run out on him, and there had seemed only one way to save his pride in front of all those people at the church; the newspaper photographers and well-wishers; the acquaintances and the enemies that men of power made for themselves.

She had dressed in the white lace gown and adjusted the long antique veil over her face. Downstairs in the hall Uncle Dominic had stood waiting. 'You're beautiful,' he had said, and he was too overwrought on this his daughter's wedding day to realize that he kissed his niece and led her on his arm to the waiting wedding car.

Not a soul seemed to question the supposed absence of Fenny from the wedding. Everyone had always known that she was shy; it had always been a family joke ... a jest without laughter, for today she had posed as her cousin and there at the altar of the Greek church she had been wedded to a man who had barely noticed her existence ... until this astounding moment.

'How on earth did you get away with it?' He swung her forward and gripped her hair in his angry fist, raking his eyes over her face. 'It was that infernal veil, eh? Behind that virginal yashmak you looked like her, but pale and nervous on this of all days. It was an added touch of

7

cleverness, my bride, to feel faint in the vestry and be too overcome to attend the reception.

'Tell me,' he leaned closer to her and his eyes seemed to have a volcanic fury burning away inside them, 'do you feel so clever now you're alone with me – at our honeymoon hotel?'

Fenny felt the pain of her stretched scalp where he gripped her hair in his fist, but most of all she felt a terrible guilt, and an equally awful sense of fear. Heraklion Mavrakis was pure Greek and that fact had aided and abetted this entire masquerade.

He had driven in a separate car to the hotel, with his two brothers and a couple of business associates, for almost like Arabs these men didn't associate with women in public. Women were their private affair, and so she had been kept apart from him until this moment when they faced each other entirely alone – husband and bride.

Each separate moment of that morning now seemed as sharply etched on Fenny's mind as the facets of the emerald ring which Penela had left on the dressing-table of her bedroom, resting on the folded, hastily written note which she had left for someone – anyone to give to the Greek she had met in Athens, while doing one of the many odd jobs she undertook while she waited for small parts in the theatre. Being courier to a coachload of holidaymakers suited Penela, for she had a scintillating manner and was shy of no one.

That was how she had attracted the man who now stood with Fenny in the luxurious sitting-room of the Parkway Towers in London. An attraction which must have struck deep, for it was fairly well known that Greeks preferred to marry their own kind of women, reared to the traditional ideas of the country.

It would have taken a great deal of attraction to have

brought him to England to ask of Dominic Odell the hand of his only daughter.

But the hand which Heraklion Mavrakis had held in church that morning had been Fenny's, and it was upon her marriage finger that he had slid the engraved band of purest gold, glinting in the sunlight through the peaked windows above the altar. A similar but wider band of gold had been placed by her shaking fingers upon his right hand ... even yet she could remember how she had trembled, almost dropping the ring as she dared the wrath of the gods and the Greek himself by standing there in the guise of the girl he really wanted.

The lovely wedding gown had been trimmed with Virgin's Flower, and it had crossed Fenny's mind to wonder if her cousin had run from Lion more in fear than in any real urgency to undertake this understudy role in New York.

Fenny knew of the affair which Penela had had with Drake Montressen, the producer. Since their schooldays Fenny had acted as the recipient of her cousin's secrets, and having no family of her own she had been grateful to be treated almost like a sister by the volatile Penela. Even Dominic Odell, who was a successful commercial artist, would have been shocked had he known that his beloved only child had given herself to a man like Montressen, years older than Penela, a hard drinker and frank womanizer.

Fenny had tried to hide her own sense of shock ... yet who was she to condemn a passing affair with a man, when she had done something that was almost blasphemous! Clad in a wedding veil not her own, she had gone through the ritual of a Greek wedding, circling the altar three times with the groom, joined to him by the ribbons of the flowered coronets. Then she had sipped the wedding wine and kissed the Silver Bible printed in beautiful Greek script. A ceremony that was sacred in Greek eyes, binding and only to be shorn by the blade of death.

Under the skirts of the lace gown the satin slip had rustled as if she walked through leaves, and under the folds of the veil she had known that her face was as white as the flowers trimming the gown, the tiny lilies of the valley, symbolic of a virgin, in body, heart and mind.

Flowers that might have been symbolic of Fenny, before she had deceived a man in a church.

A vein beat at his temple as he gazed down at her, and never in her life had she seen anyone look so furious. He looked as if he could have gripped his hands around her neck and choked the breath out of her, and she wouldn't have blamed him. She might even have welcomed her release from a situation which grew more frightening with every passing second.

'How could you dare to stand in her shoes and take on her name—?'

'I didn't,' Fenny said, and the words barely scraped past her rigid lips. 'I – I declared my own name, which sounds like hers—'

'Cousin Fenny!' His mouth looked savage and she saw the contemptuous anger flare in his eyes.

'Fenella,' she whispered. 'I – I even wrote it in the register, and you could have said there and then that I was a fake.'

'Your hand was shaking so much that you could have signed yourself Jezebel and it would hardly have been decipherable – I must say I wondered that Penela seemed so nervous, but why should I suspect that the girl at my side, her fair hair gleaming through the wedding veil, was other than my real bride? Why should I suspect a figure of sham – or should I say shame?'

He glowered down at her and Fenny gave a nervous shudder as his fingers dug painfully into the fine bones of her shoulder. He pulled her over to the window, where the late afternoon sunlight was spilling into the room, unrestrained because they were so high up in the penthouse suite of the hotel.

'Now I see that you aren't even a replica of her,' he said cuttingly. 'But the devil knows that most brides take on a look which is different from their everyday appearance. Even relatives and friends are subdued by that air of strangeness which she has, for the face behind the veil seems a stranger's face and a man wonders if he is being wed to a figure of wax and blossom. Where the hands had been warm in his, they are cold and tremulous at the altar. Where the voice had been seductive, it takes on a cool and distant note—

'Saints in purgatory, how is a man to be sure at the altar itself that he is marrying, in the shape of this snow maiden, the same woman who melted in his arms the night before!'

Fenny cried out then, for his grip had become a torment, and everything about him was strange and cruel. She had never been alone with him before; she had only seen and known him across a crowded room, the Greek fiancé of her cousin, who had the height of a Guardsman, the sinewy power of a knife dancer, and the eyes of a tiger.

'If I am hurting you, then you've asked for it.' Those eyes raked over her, densely amber, combined with scimitar brows that met blackly above his hard-boned nose. Lines were deeply incised beside his mouth, and only during the ceremony had his voice been as darkly sensuous as rough Greek wine and crusted honey. Now it was like a knife cutting into her.

'There is plenty of pain in store for you, little fake.' It

was a promise, not a threat. 'You can't have expected any pleasure when you put on that white dress and concealed your face behind that infernal veil! Tell me, what did you expect when you stepped into Penela's shoes?'

His eyes probed for the truth, and Fenny had to thrust it far down out of sight in the deep recesses of her heart, desperately aware that if he caught a glimpse of that incredible truth he would drag it forth and tear it to pieces.

Let him believe the obvious – that being poor she had seen the opportunity of becoming rich and so she had taken a gamble which had paid off. He would understand that, but never the real reason why she had masqueraded as Penela ... that one evening across her uncle's lounge she had looked at Lion Mavrakis and felt her bones turn to water. She had thought that such a sensation belonged only to fear, but for hours that night she had lain awake, haunted by images of him that made her bury her face in the pillows.

Pushing a hand into a pocket of Penela's suit, she drew forth the note which her cousin had hastily scrawled before running out on him. Silently she handed it to him, knowing each word that he read in total silence.

Dear Lion, it ran,

In a way I'm still crazy about you, and I know we could have had exciting times together, but I want to be an actress and you as a Greek would never permit me to have such a career. I have the chance to understudy Gertrude Maine in New York, in a super new play, and I just can't turn it down.

Please try to understand, and for the sake of loving me, which I know you do, please try to forgive me for running out on you.

Fenny will probably give you this note. She can be trusted to be discreet, and you can always tell other people that we had a quarrel.

Thanks for the memories. Your truant, Penela.

Fenny winced as the silence was broken by the crackling of the paper in his fist as he crushed the note into a ball and tossed it into the wastepaper basket near the bureau. That was that, the gesture seemed to say. A wasted courtship, a love not worth having, the end of smiling indulgence towards a pretty young thing.

'So you can be trusted, eh?' His narrowed eyes dwelt on Fenny, hard and dangerous in his present mood, that of a man of command who had been jilted by one girl and outrageously fooled by another. Fenny's heart felt cold and heavy as a stone, for she knew that he would never forgive her.

'W-what are you going to do?' She had to ask him, she had to know his intentions, for in too many ways he was a stranger to her and she couldn't be sure if he meant to throw her out of this suite in which, ironically, she was both a bride and an interloper.

'What would you like me to do?' His tone of voice was infinitely mocking. 'You know better than I why you came to the church in all the finery of another woman and with demure audacity went through with what she ran out on. The penniless little cousin, eh? Who always sat in the corner with the family cat! Do you realize how completely at my mercy you are?'

'I – I think so.' Fenny stood there in the beautifully cut sapphire blue suit, braced against the anger that simmered in every sinew of that tall, lean, hard-muscled body in dark grey suiting. His very stillness was more of a menace than a restless show of anger would have been. His face looked more than ever as if it had been forged in the furnaces of Sparta . . . too forbidding to be handsome; too striking ever to be forgotten.

'I could throw you from that window, and who would

blame me? Who would care?'

'No one,' she admitted. 'You'd be justified.'

'I'm gratified that you realize it.' His eyes swept her up and down. 'I'm still astounded that I could have been fooled into believing that I was marrying Penela. Where she sparkles, you are reserved. Your eyes are smoky blue, while hers are sapphire. Your hair is gold and not platinum, and you have not the seductive curve to the mouth. Do you know exactly how I feel about you?'

'I can guess,' Fenny said quietly, and never in her life had anything hurt like the look of sheer blazing contempt in the amber eyes of this man who was legally her husband.

'I doubt if any girl, even you, has the imagination to plumb the depths of what I feel when I look at you.' His voice seemed to crackle with shards of frozen ice. 'It's as if I purchased a diamond and arrived home to find myself with a piece of paste. I feel robbed, *kyria,* and that is an emotion that no Greek can tolerate.'

'I – I'm sorry,' she managed to say. Her throat felt dry and her head was hot and achy. What she had done, and what she had got away with, was like an incredible dream from which she wanted to awake, but the dream clung and when she looked into Lion's eyes it held elements of nightmare from which she had to run.

She glanced from him to the door, desperately. Yes, if she could get out into the corridor she might just escape the retribution of a Greek who felt, justifiably, that he had been cheated.

She moved abruptly, heading for the door, but she forgot that the shoes she was wearing were not her own and even as she grabbed at the door handle she stumbled and one of the shoes flew off her foot, the cardboard sole dropping out on the carpet. Hands caught at her, biting into her as they lifted her and carried her to the wide sofa where she was unceremoniously dropped to the cushions, breathless and frightened. She gazed up at him, her smoky eyes filled with distress, and a pleading which had no effect on his pitiless face, for in no way did the dark features soften or the eyes that swept her up and down. He reached out and as she shrank from him, he jerked the other shoe from her right foot and flung it across the room.

'So the slipper doesn't fit Cinderella,' he said, with mockery. 'And you might as well know, here and now, that I'm no Prince Charming who will be gallant and gracious enough to let you go now you have kindly "saved my face" as you no doubt think of it. You little fool, do you think I care about the opinion of those who come to watch weddings and aim their cameras at a man because he happens to have a good head for business and so makes money at it? I was marrying Penela because she held out for that — do you understand me? She sparkled like a gem and I wanted her — in her place I have you, and there is nothing either of us can do about it.'

'Oh, but there is.' Fenny wanted above all to put right the wrong that she had done, acting so impulsively, so crazily, driven by feelings that even her fear of him couldn't entirely subdue. 'The marriage can be annulled and then you'll be free—'

'A Greek marriage?' His face was cruelly sardonic. 'Did you suppose that because I came to your country to marry your cousin I did so with the idea that if it didn't work out we could sever the bonds as if they were made of silk instead of steel? Look at me! I am a Spartan by birth and I don't profess to be a saint, but I do abide by the laws of my church. Do you understand what that means?'

Fenny could feel each hammering stroke of her heart as she sat there among silk cushions on the saffron couch, her eyes fixed upon the dark, relentless face of this man from Sparta ... this man fashioned from tempered steel whom she dared – oh God, whom she dared to love!

'It means,' he said deliberately, 'that you and I are forged together until one of us dies, and right now I could more easily be rid of you if I broke your neck.'

'Oh no!' she gasped, and if possible her face whitened, almost to a marble hue so that her eyes were like great smoke-filled shadows in her distress.

'Scared that I'll do it?' he sneered. 'Relax, my dear, you aren't worth a long stretch in prison, least of all a Greek cell. Well, like it or not, I have a wife and we might as well open the champagne which Zonar brought to the hotel.'

She watched dumbly as he went to the bar and took hold of the bottle which his brother had placed in the ice-pail. She had stood by the window, her back to the brothers while they had jested with Lion. 'Good luck!' the youngest, Zonar, had called out to her. '*Avrio*, new sister!'

Until tomorrow, when they would be flying to Greece to the island of Petaloudes, which had become the property of Lion Mavrakis, owner of marble quarries, vineyards, fig terraces, an olive-oil factory, a fish-canning business, cargo caiques, a couple of hotels, a nightclub, three restaurants and some spacious villas. He was said to speculate in everything. To be both charitable, and stony hard. At the close of the war he and his small brothers had been among the many orphans grubbing for an existence. They had survived because Lion was tough, ruthless and brainy ... Fenny hadn't dared to face those brothers who adored him, throwing compliments and laughter at him as they left him alone with her, to enjoy his wedding night.

Her nerves quivered as the champagne cork leapt from

the bottle and fell to the carpet near the couch where she huddled.

'Aren't you going to pick it up – for luck?' he asked, in that deep voice which held that awful grating contempt for her and what she had done to get him. He would never truly believe that she had wanted to save his pride ... he was too self-sufficient and realistic ever to understand that a woman might care for him without ever being close to him. All his life he had taken what he wanted; grasped, grappled and fought for a firm position in the world, and all he would ever feel with regard to her was a deep and abiding anger that something he didn't want had been foisted on to him ... a woman whom he must call his wife.

He came towards her with a pair of brimming wine glasses in his hands. The champagne was a pale topaz with bubbles clinging to the edges of the stemmed glasses ... the wine of celebration, for those who had joy in their hearts instead of bitterness.

As he came to her, he deliberately kicked the cork out of his way and it rolled under the couch. So much for luck, she thought. He didn't expect to have any where she was concerned.

'Here you are.' He held one of the glasses towards her, and she could feel a harsh lump in her throat as she accepted the champagne, her murmur of thanks hardly audible.

'And what shall we drink to?' he asked. 'Long life and great pleasure in each other's loving company?'

'Don't,' she pleaded. 'You make me feel – criminal.'

'That is what you are, *kyria*. You have stolen what was meant for another woman.'

'But Penela ran out on you—'

'I should have followed her, you little fool. That is what she hoped for, that I'd jump into the Alouette and go after her and prove to her that marriage to me could be more exciting than standing in the wings of a theatre watching someone else take the kisses of the crowd.' He lifted his glass and took a deep swig of his wine. 'Life can be even more dramatic than a play, but I don't much care for a role which has been thrust upon me. I don't care for the leading lady I have to act with!'

The champagne glass trembled in Fenny's hand and the lump in her throat was so painful that she had to drink to ease it.

'Drink deeply,' he said, that biting edge to his voice, 'you're going to need the courage. *Stin iyia sou!*'

Her eyes clung to his face as if mesmerized. 'Cheers!' he mocked. 'Isn't that what the English say when they take a drink with someone? By the Virgin, I look at you and wonder how you found the nerve to play such a game with me. What was it you wanted – you have no home of your own, I understand?'

'Uncle Dominic lets me have a room in their house,' she said huskily, feeling no self-pity but only a shocked wonder that she was here in this expensive hotel suite with this man who was actually her husband. Some primitive female instinct had driven her to take Penela's place, and now she was a prisoner of her own crazy impulse.

'The traditional poor relation, eh? The plain little mouse eaten up with envy of her pretty cousin, who grabbed the cheese with a smart snap of her teeth as soon as the opportunity offered.' He went to the bar, taking long lithe strides, his body giving off a sort of controlled energy. He took the champagne bottle in his hand, refilled his own glass and brought the bottle across to Fenny. 'Hold out your glass! Come! Only the haze of this stuff will help us to face this mad situation, for face it we must. To a Greek a betrothal is binding, let alone a marriage. We break neither!'

As he poured wine into her glass some of it splashed from the brim, and his lips moved in a cruel little smile. 'Spilled wine is supposed to bring luck, but in this case it has brought misfortune, though as a Greek I have my share of affinity with the ironic shades that lurk around the corners of life.

'Drink!' he ordered. 'Wine should descend impetuously, like thunder.'

She shuddered and obeyed his order, feeling the strong wine rise to her head, but aware that it might cushion her against the cutting remarks he had every right to make. He still wanted Penela and she had frustrated him in his desire... the plain little mouse, he had called her, who had snatched the cheese meant for her cousin.

Little tremors of nervous reaction were running through her as she watched him pace back and forth across the carpet, and she knew that it was his pride, not his nerves, that were affected by the discovery that he was married to the wrong woman. He had too much *zoikos*, too vital a temperament and toughness to be shattered by the situation, but Fenny could feel the anger that simmered in his lean hard body, and whenever he glanced at her she shrank a little more from the tigerish, brow-shaded eyes.

He would find a way to punish her, and she must accept that punishment because she had earned it.

'Take that hat off,' he said curtly. 'You're staying here, you know.'

Her nerves quivered as he flung the words at her, then she set aside her wine glass and with unsteady hands she took off the small, grey suede hat and placed it on the sofa table. She shook out her hair, a soft gold frame about the sensitivity of her face, set with the smoke-coloured eyes that had a Celtic slant to them, the thick lashes tipped with the gold of her hair. She wasn't obviously attractive like Penela, but there was a subtle quality to her face. He had called her plain to be cruel, but as she sat there, the reddening sunlight across her skin, she felt him staring at her with narrowed eyes.

'Quite the tortured angel, aren't you?' he sneered.

'And you are the iron pirate, aren't you?' She had deeply offended him, and cheated him out of what he wanted, but she wasn't quite without a dash of spirit. 'No heart, so no forgiveness.'

'None,' he agreed, leaning there against the bar. 'Did you expect me to forgive you? Then your optimism must match your opportunism.'

'I'm certainly not optimistic in that respect,' she said. 'I fully realize how much you must – hate me.'

'Oh yes, *kyria,* we Greeks can hate very thoroughly. Do you look forward to being the recipient of a man's devoted hatred in place of his tender love?'

'So – so you are going to let the marriage stand?' Her hands clenched in her lap and she had to fight not to leap up and make another attempt to reach that door. He would be after her like a big cat on a mouse if she tried it, and she knew that his temper was frayed to the edge of physical violence.

'Do you know what we say in Greece? When disaster comes the stars go dark – yes, you will be my wife, and I shall make you regret every moment of that deception at the altar of my church. Greek marital laws are not slack like your English ones. Once we take vows, we keep them, and I vow to make you sorry every day that you draped yourself in Penela's veil and wore it to deceive me. You made a mockery of that veil, hiding yourself behind it in order to play thief, liar and harlot!'

'Oh no,' she gasped. 'That's unfair!'

'It's the only truth of this entire day. You stole your cousin's place at my side, you lied your way through the ceremony, and you will complete your harlotry when you lie in my arms tonight and give yourself to me.'

'No!' She leapt to her feet. 'I never meant any of this to get out of hand. I only meant to save your pride—'

'Really? Do you think there is pride in a man who finds himself wedded to a woman he never wanted?'

'No—' Fenny swayed where she stood. 'Y-you'd have stood there, waiting for Penela. It would have been humiliating for you—'

'And is this situation less so, that I find myself the husband of a woman for whom I haven't a scrap of feeling – except that of contempt? Well, the damage is done and can't be undone. You now have my name and whatever my feelings with regard to you, I won't have that name smirched by a lot of gossip. We Greeks live our lives with honour.'

'To the outside world?' she asked, feeling as if at any moment her legs would give way and she would fall to the floor in front of him. She couldn't do that. She had to fight her way out of this room, and if she couldn't do it physically, then she must try and do it with persuasion. 'I never meant to hurt your pride, believe me. I only – oh, I know it was a mad, bad thing to do, but—'

'I think you knew exactly what you were doing, and meant to do from the moment that you read Penela's note. You knew I had money, and your cousin would have told you about my *kastello* on the island. How much more satisfying to have an entire house instead of a single room, and what a small price to pay, the giving of your body to the rough, self-made Greek who being what he is must be honoured to have the slim white shape of an

21

English girl in his arms.'

'I – I never thought any such thing,' she protested, yet even so the confused blood rose in her cheeks as there came a swift recollection of that night when she had lain awake thinking of him, so unlike the other men who had hung around Penela, who attracted them as a bright lamp the big and the small moths. Could she truly deny that it had not crossed her mind to wonder what it felt like to be close to that strength that was like sculptured rock, from the long black brows to the long legs, with something excitingly ruthless about his mouth and lean jawline?

'Well, if you've been curious about me, *kyria,* then I promise to satisfy that curiosity.' His strong-looking hands made an expressive movement, and the eyes that he fixed upon her looked as hard as slithers of steel. 'As we say in Greece, "no woman should live like a fruitless fig tree", and so you might as well earn your Greek bread and your lodging. You have good health, eh? You're a trifle on the coltish side, but your skin is clear and your teeth look good—'

'I'm not a damned horse!' she suddenly flung at him, stung by the way he was regarding her. 'I did what I did from the best of good intentions, but I'm not staying around to be insulted by you—'

'You are going to do exactly what I tell you.' And as he spoke he began to move towards her, until she was backing away from the towering strength of him, acutely aware of being alone with him in this penthouse suite into which no outsiders would intrude on them ... a honeymoon couple. In her shoeless feet she felt so much smaller than he, her toes clenching the carpet as she found herself backed up against the long silk curtains at the windows, beyond which the day was darkening.

Trapped there, a slim figure in her borrowed blue, she gave a small broken cry as he caught hold of her and jerked her against the dark grey smoothness of his jacket.

'You chose to marry me and in so doing you cut yourself free of your uncle, and you are now my sole property, to do with exactly as I please.' His eyes fixed hers and his hands bit into her waist. 'Do I make myself explicit enough for you?'

'Oh yes.' Fenny couldn't keep the tremor from her voice, or her legs. 'Your English is excellent, *kyrie*. You are going to make me abide by those vows I made so madly—'

'I think you made them quite deliberately, having weighed the gains against the losses. What, after all, had you to lose? A back bedroom in the home of your relatives and being in the shadow of your more dazzling cousin.'

'Y-you imagine I was jealous of Penela?' Fenny gazed up at him with indignant eyes. 'It just isn't true and you have no right to imply it.'

'You are the one without the rights,' he said curtly. 'I am a Greek and even Penela would not have had all her own way with me, but you – you are like the brides of Sparta, to be used for only one purpose!'

Her face lost every vestige of colour, for his face was as hard and dark as if chiselled from Spartan rock. 'W–what do you mean?'

'Aren't you woman enough to know what I mean?' His hands tightened and every inch of her was pressed against him, leaving no space between them and no room in her heart for any doubt that the mercy of a Greek would not be tender.

'Y-you have every right to be angry and you must believe that I'm truly s-sorry for what I did.' The trembling in her legs had crept up her body and Fenny knew, with mortification, that he could feel her nervous tremors.

23

'Please won't you let me go before we end up hating the sight of each other? Things can be put right between you and Penela, if you still love her.'

'Love?' A black brow arched with infinite sarcasm. 'I have never wasted that emotion on any woman, you little fool.'

'But you said – you told me you'd have gone after Penela.'

'And so I should, but what in the name of heaven has that to do with love? I wanted her! Do you understand what that means, or are you more fool than knave?'

The wild colour flooded back into Fenny cheeks as the implication in his words struck her. *But you didn't have to marry Penela for that.* The words cried through her mind as she recalled her cousin's confession that she had allowed herself to be seduced by Drake Montressen at a quaint inn at Stratford-on-Avon. Then, afraid that something of her thoughts might show in her eyes, Fenny dropped her gaze to Lion's wide shoulders. How firm and strong they looked, so that it would have been heaven to lean her tired head against them ... but she didn't have the right ... she didn't have anything but his contempt.

'Look at me!' With cruel insistence he gripped her hair and forced back her head so he could search her eyes. 'You placed yourself on the altar – made a personal sacrifice of yourself, so don't act the frightened virgin at this stage of the game. So you want to live in a *kastello*, on my island in the Aegean – so be it! In exchange for those you will give me a son, and you will do it within the year, and when I have the boy, then and only then will I release you from this marriage. Do you hear me, little fake?'

She heard him in a kind of dazed wonder ... in exchange for her freedom she must have his baby, and the child must be a boy ... like some pagan god of olden times he asked this of her, as if her terror and torment would automatically produce a son for him.

'Aren't you being impossibly arrogant?' she asked, a flicker of pain across her face as she felt the pull of his fingers in her hair. 'What if I can't have a baby – or it turns out to be a girl?'

Then, before he could answer her, Fenny gave a broken laugh.

'Will you break my neck, *kyrie*?'

His eyes raked over her face, dusky-gold and dangerous between the black lashes. 'We must hope that you can bear a child and that it is a boy. I don't think you'd care to spend a second year on Petaloudes with a man who merely wants to make use of you.'

When he said that Fenny shivered so convulsively in his arms that her teeth chattered ... suddenly she was shaking like an aspen and couldn't control the spasms. The trauma of the day had hold of her and she was like someone in the grip of a fever as the powerful arms swung her upwards and carried her to the couch. This time she was lowered to the cushions, and as she huddled there, shaking coldly, she vaguely heard him speaking on the telephone.

'Room service.' His voice was brisk with authority, with not a hint of softening towards her distress. 'Please bring hot coffee and breast of turkey sandwiches to the penthouse suite,' he ordered.

There was a ting as the receiver was replaced, and a moment later he was bending over Fenny. 'Pull yourself together, for I won't tolerate such a show of nerves – if they are genuine. In all probability you're in need of nourishment, as you weren't at the reception. A waiter is bringing some food for you, so for heaven's sake get hold of yourself.'

Fenny tried desperately to do as he asked, but her skin burned beneath the scorn of his eyes and her nerves felt as if they were shaking her body to pieces. She clutched a cushion to her in an effort to control the shivers, and she tried to look away from him, but was held inexorably by the strange ring of gold around each dense pupil of his eyes. It gave to his glance an added menace ... he meant every word that he had said to her about the marriage ... he was a Greek and he had struck a bargain, and he would make her abide by it.

There came a discreet knock at the door, and then it opened and a waiter wheeled a service trolley into the sitting-room. Lion immediately stepped in front of Fenny so that his powerful frame half-concealed her from the waiter's glance.

'*Evkaristo*,' he said, and he stood there unmoving until the door closed and they were left alone once more. Then he approached the trolley and there came to Fenny the sound and aroma of coffee being poured. He brought the cup to her. 'Come!' He said it as if he were speaking to an obstinate donkey. 'Stop acting the child, for it cuts no ice with me, I can assure you. Drink the coffee and then you will eat a couple of sandwiches and feel less foolish.'

'W-what a sympathetic man you are.' She dropped the cushion and took the cup of coffee from his hand. It slopped a little and she winced as the hot liquid splashed on to her knee. She bent her head and put her shaking lips to the brim and found that he had well sugared the coffee though he had left out the cream. She drank steadily, concentrating on getting it down her dry throat, as desirous of throwing off the shakes as he was insistent that she do so. He evidently took her for a thorough actress and she really couldn't blame him. She had earned every fraction of his scorn and dislike, but all she had wanted to do was silence the voices of speculation and gossip when

Penela failed to appear at his side in her wedding white. Men such as Lion were bound to make enemies, and they'd have crowed to see him left standing alone at the altar ... a Greek to whom *philotemo* was just about everything; the absolute male pride of a people who had never bowed their heads to tyrants or toil. They had an indestructible quality, and it was that in Heraklion Mavrakis which had drawn Fenny to his side in place of her runaway cousin.

'Now can you eat a sandwich or two?' he asked, taking from her hand the cup which she had emptied to the coffee grounds.

'I – I'm not sure.' Fenny felt weak, but he was mostly to blame for that. 'I suppose I could try.'

'You will certainly try.' He went to the trolley and placed a couple of sandwiches on a plate, along with a tomato and some crisp leaves of lettuce. His face was iron, and his eyes a cold saffron as he handed the plate of food to Fenny.

'Thank you.' Her voice was husky. 'Aren't you going to have some?'

'I might as well. We shall be dining in the restaurant at seven-thirty, and then I have seats at the Aldwych for the new production of *Hamlet*. I don't know whether you are a fan of the Bard, but Penela was, and it was at her suggestion that we attend the play.'

Fenny gave an uncontrollable start when he mentioned her cousin's fondness for Shakespeare, for that addiction was bound up in her mind with Penela's affair with Drake Montressen, who now and again produced a season of the Master's plays. It had occurred to Fenny to wonder if her cousin had gone off to New York to play understudy at his suggestion. A man like Montressen didn't let go of his conquests very easily, not when they were as attractive as Penela. There was no denying that Penela wanted to be a successful actress, and Lion was altogether too much a Greek to entertain the idea of his wife displaying herself on a stage for other men to admire ... and desire.

'Do you like Shakespeare?' she asked Lion, aware of how little she knew of his preferences; how far from intimate was her knowledge of this man who meant to enforce those marriage vows she had spoken as in a dream ... a dream she had never meant to become a painful reality.

'I can take him or leave him, depending on my mood.' Lion had dropped into an armchair with sandwiches of his own, and when he bit into one of them, Fenny followed his example and found the turkey meat tender and appetizing. Hunger stirred awake in her young body, for she hadn't eaten a thing all day, all thought of food wiped from her mind from the moment she had found that note of Penela's, propped up against a scent bottle with her emerald engagement ring. It hadn't been quite in character for her to leave the ring behind, but Fenny had cynically guessed that her cousin was more than a little afraid of the man she had jilted.

How could a woman jilt Lion like that, especially when he had shown Penela how much he wanted her? Hadn't he said that last night she had melted in his arms!

Fenny shivered again as she pictured how it would be for her in his arms ... arms without any protective tenderness in their embrace, but bonds of steel about her, enforcing her obedience to what he demanded of her body. Only when she placed a son in his arms would he hand her the key to her freedom ... until that moment she was bound to him ... loving him yet fearing every hard, proud, sun-weathered sinew of him.

The turkey meat stuck in her throat and she swallowed convulsively. She lowered her eyes and fought back the tears that threatened. He wouldn't be moved to see her weeping, no more than he had pitied her in the grip of that shaking panic.

'I – I wish I could make you believe how sorry I am.' Her voice was little more than a whisper. 'I acted on impulse—'

'You acted superbly,' he drawled. 'Please, spare me any more tear-jerking explanations. You have brought off a *coup de théatre* that a Bernhardt might be proud of, and there really is no need to add to the performance with the appeal and shyness of a virgin hesitant on the curb of life. Are you a virgin, by the way?'

'Of course!' Her eyes widened with shock at the question.

'There is no "of course" about it, *kyria*.' He struck a match and lit a thin cigar, his eyes intent on her face as the strong smoke made patterns in the air. 'Any girl who plants herself on a man in the guise of his fiancée is too much a mistress of deceit to be altogether a little innocent. *C'est la vie!* I shall know tonight, one way or the other, shall I not?'

Colour burned in Fenny's cheeks, and she saw his lips give a sarcastic little twist. 'Eat the remainder of that food,' he ordered. 'And don't run away with the idea that I have any protective instincts where you are concerned. I am merely making sure of not having a wreck on my hands instead of a woman. Tonight we play – tomorrow we fly to Greece. You have a passport?'

She nodded and chewed a piece of sandwich that now tasted like straw in her mouth.

'Yes, I recall that Penela said you were going to take a holiday in Crete with an office companion – a man?'

'No!' Fenny gave him an indignant look. He was quick to question her morals, but did he imagine Penela had been the angel that she practised to appear, polishing the performance in front of her bedroom mirror!

'It hardly matters.' He shrugged his powerful shoulders. 'You mean nothing to me, beyond the means to an end, and I don't doubt that I should have had trouble with Penela on that score. You will have a child whether you desire one or not, for I never play at half-games.'

His words were like knives stabbing into Fenny, so aimed that each one penetrated and left her inwardly hurt. But she had her own sort of pride and she tilted her chin and steadied her voice. 'I've earned a judicious beating, but we can't live together without any affection at all – it would be hell!'

'I shall make sure that it is.' He emitted smoke from his nostrils, and his eyelids were lowered in a look of cold, hard indifference. 'Did you expect heaven from a man who thoroughly despises you? Surely not, my dear. You only had your thoughts on the material advantages, for all of Penela's luggage is here, complete with the trousseau I bought her. If her wedding gown fitted you then the rest of the wardrobe should – apart from the shoes.'

His eyes flicked her feet, curled small among the cushions of the couch, and as he looked at her Fenny could feel her toes curling together as if seeking protection from a look which said that having stepped into Penela's shoes she must now give him value for his money. Love was not involved; it was entirely a mercenary arrangement – the good life for a year in exchange for the son that was so important to the Greek male.

It meant nothing to him that she had acted in a purely emotional way, obeying a primitive impulse deep within her. He saw her only as a little cheat ... an opportunist who would have all the material things he would have given Penela, but none of the affectionate tolerance or the indulgent kindness.

It was there in his eyes what she would be ... his kept woman.

'You are being very hard – and unforgiving,' she said, with no hope in her heart that he would relent, for as he sat there with the thin cigar clenched between his teeth he looked quite merciless. The old ways of Sparta ran deep in his veins and to him she was a creature without virtue, to be used merely for his pleasure.

'It's justice that we should pay for our sins,' he said. 'Did you stupidly imagine that I would treat you like an icon, an object of my worship? The fates have worked it so I find myself your husband, and as you are a fairly presentable female I might as well make the most of you. You will dress as glamorously as your cousin, and in front of my family you will show me all the respect and close attention that a Greek requires from a new young bride.'

'You mean I must pretend to – love you?' He wasn't to know, she thought achingly, that love for him was the only reality of a day of pretence.

'Yes, and you will make as good a show of it as you made at the altar today. I am the head of the family, all responsibilities and burdens are mine, and in the way of a Greek household I have the respect and awe of my brothers – it is my right to expect it from you – my wife!'

Wife ... the word sent a shock of feeling through Fenny. The strange dream shattered and the reality swept over her. She was indeed the wife of Heraklion Mavrakis, unsought by him but accepted on his own uncompromising terms.

There he sat, dark and stern, her judge in the guise of a husband, her tormentor, not her lover. She curled down smaller among the cushions as if seeking to hide herself from what she saw in his eyes.

'I take it you have had the necessary jabs for a trip abroad?' he asked. 'There are wild dogs in the hills of

Greece, used by the shepherd lads for keeping their flocks together, and a bite from one of them can be dangerous.'

'Would it matter?' Fenny felt at this moment as if nothing could be so mortally painful as being dispised by Lion.

'Of course, you little fool.' He breathed out smoke with an impatient air of contempt. 'Hydrophobia is even more unpleasant than a loveless marriage, for it happens to be fatal. You have had your jabs?'

'Yes,' she admitted, and knew how hopeless was a lie, for he suddenly towered to his feet, came across to her with those long strides, and reached down to remove the jacket of the blue suit.

'Show me your arm,' he ordered, and she quivered, feeling his touch on her skin as he pushed up the silky sleeve of the white blouse. Her skin was pale in his dark fingers and she gave a slight wince as he ran his fingertips across the bruising from the needles. 'With a little liar for a wife I have to check up on you, eh? What of your passport and papers? Have you brought them with you, or are they at your uncle's house?'

'They're in my handbag.' Still he was holding her arm, and she could feel his touch right through to her bones, sending the most acute sensations to the nerve centres in her rib region ... the rib said to have been taken from Adam for the creation of Eve. It had been but a myth until Fenny experienced for herself those strange little pangs that made her want to gasp.

'You left nothing to chance, did you?' He stared down at her. 'What made you want to visit Crete?'

'I – I had heard it was a fascinating place.'

'So it is, but Petaloudes is even more so. Its cliffs are the colour of henna, created from a volcanic eruption of the seabed itself. The *kastello* is built high, erected in the days of Turkish occupation for the pasha of the island – the position which I now hold, you might say. No doubt your cousin spoke to you about the island and that is when you began to feel covetous—'

'No—' Fenny shook her head and wished she might convince him of her sincerity. 'I've never been covetous of anything relating to Penela, and you must believe me. What happened today had a sort of – oh, I don't know how to explain. When I found myself in the church it was too late to do anything but make the responses—'

'I will see to it that you make all the responses.' His smile was wholly cynical as he lowered a knee to the couch and suddenly bent right over her. She felt his hands close around her neck, holding her still while he explored her lips for the first time. The disturbing intimacy made her feel faint. She knew how much he could make her suffer, and she felt lost in the dark centre of the storm she had stirred up.

'You don't kiss at all like your cousin.' His hands cupped her head and her hair spilled down over his fingers as he gazed down into her eyes, his expression both mocking and curious. 'What the devil are you – an ineffable innocent, or the cleverest little bitch that ever got born? A nereid, perhaps, who appears to man in the diaphanous veil of mock-modesty. Whatever the truth, it is no use for a man to look for sparks in yesterday's fire. I must make the most of you.'

Then, as if fury surged through him anew that he should be holding her and not Penela, his hands tightened about her throat as if he came very close to breaking her neck. 'There are hair-fine lines between most things – love and hate – rapture and rape, and, by the gods, you and I are going to tread a very thin tightrope between them. Are you prepared for that?'

'I have to be,' she said faintly. 'You give me no choice.'

'None, my little fake. Not a hope on earth that I shall let you go until you give me the only thing I want from you – a black-haired, bawling son for Lion Mavrakis!'

CHAPTER TWO

It was a Doric-styled dress, sleeveless, with a band of embroidery below the bosom where it fell in chiffon panels to an embroidered hem. There was no doubt that it had been especially designed for Penela, but because Fenny had a similarity of shape, height and fairness the dress also seemed to be made for her. The colour was ocean-blue, with deeper tones of blue in the deep bands of embroidery.

Fenny stood there in front of the mirror and felt a total stranger to herself. She had always worn neat clothes rather than striking ones, partly because her salary didn't run to them, and now with quickened beatings of her heart she saw what the ravishing prettiness of the blue dress did for her – it emphasized the fine whiteness of her skin, the smoky depths of her eyes, and the gold of her hair. She had never thought of herself as being as attractive as Penela, who had always been blessed with a total lack of inhibition which made her sparkle in the company of men, but Fenny wasn't displeased by the youthful vision facing her in the mirror. Lion couldn't complain that she looked a frump, and she found herself hoping that his Greek instincts would make him susceptible to the classic look which the Doric dress imparted to her.

Her left hand pressed itself to the beating pulse in her throat and the emerald ring winked madly in the lights of the dressing-table. Who at the estate agency would recognize in this beautifully dressed woman the neat and efficient Fenny Odell? The people she worked with would be stunned by the transformation ... and then her heart skipped as she realized all the outside implications of this marriage. Her uncle must be told, and Lion's brothers informed of the change of bride. It was all so complicated, and the gossip would burst like a bubble when it became known that she – always so reserved in her dealings with the opposite sex – was the girl who had flown off with Lion Mavrakis in his scarlet helicopter.

And then she tautened as a sound reached her from the door that connected with Lion's room. She was staring into the mirror at the reflection of the door as it swung open and his tall figure stepped into her room, assuming the privilege and freedom of a husband to invade the privacy of a wife.

'Are you ready?' he asked. 'We don't want to rush through our dinner in order to get to the theatre on time.'

'I'm almost ready.' She took up the scent spray and because of her nervousness used it rather lavishly. The delicious aroma of French perfume filled the room, and she saw the quirking of a black brow as Lion stood there, a hand lightly at rest in a pocket of his evening coat. His suit was of dark midnight-blue, worn with a white silk shirt and a narrow tie. He looked utterly foreign in his perfectly cut English suit. His distinction was of an alarming sort, he was so dark, brooding and powerful in this feminine room.

'Turn round,' he ordered. 'Let me look at you.'

She obeyed him without protest, and despite her awareness that she looked nice, she knew that he would compare her to Penela. She didn't doubt that her cousin would have added a sensuous quality to the blue dress.

With great deliberation he looked her over, until his eyes finally rested on her golden hair cut *coeur de lion* about her well-shaped head.

"The devil came, wearing the form and brightness of

an angel.'' ' He drawled the quotation in his most sardonic voice, but beyond that he wasn't going to compliment her. 'On anyone else that dress might look quite sexy.'

She knew he was referring to Penela, but she didn't rise to the gibing note in his voice. 'Don't you think I had better phone Uncle Dominic?' she asked. 'He'll be getting anxious—'

'What, about you? My impression was that the Odells rather took you for granted, along with the family cat.'

'Please – can't we be friends?' she pleaded. 'Can't we be that, at least?'

'Friendship is quite out of the question, *kyria,* so forget it.' He began to cross the carpet towards her, and Fenny had to fight with herself not to retreat from him. She must hold on to what pride she had left and meet him as bravely as she knew how. It was the only way to win some remnant of his respect, for Greeks were known to like courage and endurance. Fenny held her head high and endured his closer scrutiny.

'How you'll suffer, my sweet,' he seemed to enjoy the thought, for a deep gleam came into his dusky-gold eyes. 'You aren't of the stuff that martyrs are made – steel, wool and vinegar. What pale skin you have, as if you've always protected it from the sun and the sensuality of men. So astoundingly unlike to Penela, and yet you wore her shape at the altar. Are you something of a witch, I wonder?'

'You called me a clever bitch,' Fenny said. 'You wondered if I had any virtue, and now you seem unsure.'

'What man is ever completely sure where a woman is concerned? Even a saint could never fathom her mystery and her guile ... how fortunate that Penela's dresses fit you so well,' and as he spoke he stepped nearer and his hands moulded the soft chiffon to her body. He looked into her eyes that were the smoky blue shades of a declining summer's eve. 'You feel not unlike a slim, cool flower, and easy it would be to break you. You quiver, my dear. Does my touch make you afraid, or does it awake the woman in you?'

'You make me afraid,' she admitted, her voice a husky whisper.

'Of the physical pain if I should hurt you?' he asked.

'No.' She shook her head. 'I suppose I'm terrified of your – hate.'

'Hate is a terrifying emotion, isn't it, and we Greeks are rarely moderate in our emotions.' His hard fingers travelled to her throat and he fingered her skin as he had the material of the dress, as if she were a commodity instead of a person. 'The neck of a woman should be weighted down with pearls – real ones, strung on a chain strong enough to strangle her with. Stand still!'

And Fenny stood there as he took a slim black case from his pocket and sprang the catch. She couldn't suppress the little gasp that she gave, for there on a bed of black velvet was a coiled necklace of big milky pearls, with a clasp of tiny diamonds. He took them from the case, which he tossed to one side, and he moved round behind Fenny. This time she did attempt to retreat. 'No!' she exclaimed.

'Yes,' he contradicted. 'Stop jibbing like a little mare who feels the spur.'

'I can't wear them – they're Penela's pearls!'

'I can see no difference between wearing her dress and having these around your neck. They were bought for her, but she isn't here and you are, and it seems a pity for them to remain in a box when they can be admired against the skin of a woman. A Greek likes people to see that he can afford trinkets for his wife.'

'Trinkets?' Fenny could feel the weight of the pearls as

he fastened them. 'Aren't they real?'

'Would you like sham pearls to match your own mendacity, my little female Judas? Would it make you feel better if I said they came from Woolworth's?'

The sarcasm in his voice was enough to tell Fenny that the pearls came from a jeweller dealing only in the finest gems, for though Lion denied that he loved any woman, he had defied Greek convention to become engaged to Penela, an English girl without the traditional upbringing of a Greek; without dowry or the assured possession of her virginity. In most things Lion was entirely Greek, but the bright hair and scintillating ways of Penela had captivated him and melted his iron heart – he would never buy artificial pearls for a woman he loved, and Fenny was certain that he had loved her cousin – might still care for her despite her desertion of him on their wedding day.

He swung Fenny to face him and he gazed at the glory of the gems against her skin.

'They are what is called virgin pearls,' he told her mockingly. 'They appear to suit you, but I have no proof that they might be icing on a cake with teethmarks in it.'

'You're brutally insulting!' She wanted to tear off the pearls and fling them in his dark, taunting face. 'Are you so certain that Penela was a paragon of virtue?'

His eyes narrowed, flickering between his lashes like those of a tiger who might savage her and not feel any compunction. 'I wondered when you would get around to making insinuations about her. I said all along that you were envious of your cousin, because even in her dress and her pearls you are moonlight where she is sunlight. Your flame is that of the candle, not the lamp. Your feelings are inhibited, while hers are eager and alive. To kiss you is like putting one's lips to a piece of ice ... you react with cool calculation, not with the impulsiveness of a warm heart.'

His words fell upon Fenny like a cascade of sharp and wounding stones – he truly believed that she was everything that for years she had known Penela to be. Dazzled by her cousin, like other men, he was blinded to her love of sensation, of being the centre of attention with her sun-honeyed skin and the platinum-blonde hair that owed its stunning effectiveness to the art of a West End hairdresser. There had never been a moment in Penela's life when she hadn't put her own desires before those of anyone else – it was she who was cold and calculating at heart!

Yet Fenny couldn't say so, not without adding to the contempt Lion already felt for her. She had to accept his biased opinion of her; swallow the bitter remarks and pray that it wouldn't break her heart to be thought so little of by the man she loved.

She looked at him in silence and even as she saw the scorn of her in his striking eyes, she felt the way it weakened her knees when he touched the pearls and his fingers brushed her body.

'Put on your wrap,' he said. 'You had better start thinking of the clothes and jewels as your own, had you not?'

'If you say so, *kyrie*.'

She turned away from him and felt the shakiness of her legs as she went across to the bed, where she had laid the long, thick silk cloak with the cowl. He followed and clasped the cloak about her slender body, and she had never known before that it was possible to be aware of another human being to the very ends of her nerves. Though she looked at him with a certain fear, she felt how excitingly alive he was. She felt the dominance of his glance, the remorseless reality of being the woman he owned.

They were swept to the ground floor of the Towers,

travelling fast in the express lift. Sheathed in iron charm, Lion escorted her into the Jasmine Room, with its exotic décor and its aroma of good food. The waiter led them to a table on a little dais in an alcove, and Fenny felt sure Lion had requested such a table in advance. Let people look at them, was his attitude. Let it be known as soon as possible that in place of his publicized bride he had with him a golden-haired girl with a reserved manner.

Fenny could feel the glances of other people in the Jasmine Room, and she caught the whispers as she emerged from the cloak and the soft lights glimmered on the blue dress and the milky pearls. She and Lion were not only honeymooners; it was well known that he was a Greek magnate, but instead of the portly look of the tycoon he had the lean hardness of a man who neither drank nor ate to excess. Her own English fairness of skin and hair seemed to emphasize his Spartan darkness, and she gave a little start as he deliberately reached across the table and took hold of her hand.

'Let us give them value for their interest,' he murmured. 'Come, why not smile at your bridegroom and let everyone see how rapturously happy we are?'

'Do you have to be so cruel?' she asked.

'My dear, I have to get some pleasure out of this marriage.' With infinite mockery he carried her hand to his lips and even as he kissed her fingers, she felt him pressing her bones until they ached. The emerald ring made green lights as he moved her hand back and forth. 'A little fake from head to heel, aren't you, and I'm the proud man in possession of you.'

'You don't have to be,' she said tensely. 'Let me go—'

'When I'm ready,' he said. 'When you have paid me back in kind if not in coin. I'm a Greek and it would go against the grain of me if the terms of our bargain weren't kept to the letter. You know those terms, for I outlined them quite explicitly.'

'Do you really regard a woman whom you hate as a – a fit mother for your child?' Fenny looked at him with a tragic pride in her eyes. 'I know what you think of me.'

'Then we shall never live in any kind of doubt, *kyria*. Unlike some who go into marriage with their eyes blinded by love, we shall know that we can't suffer from disillusion.'

He released her hand and the tingling feel of it, and the way he looked at her with a twist to his lips, made her realize how much else there could be to suffer. She had to do as Lion dictated, and the more he scorched her with his sarcasm, and lashed at her pride, the more satisfied he would be.

He had justice on his side, but it was a cruel justice, and almost unaware Fenny ripped at her chiffon handkerchief as she faced him across the restaurant table. When he made love to her it would be with hate in his heart. When she had his baby he would take it away from her and put her out of his house.

'Take that dying duck expression off your face,' he ordered. 'People are looking at us.'

'I – I'm rather worried about my uncle,' she said, swallowing the painful lump in her throat. 'I should let him know where I am—'

'He knows, so you can relax.' Lion spoke curtly. 'I telephoned him an hour ago and informed him that his daughter is in New York, and his niece is with me.'

'Oh – what did he say? Did you tell him—?'

'Yes, my dear.' Lion's smile was brief and sardonic. 'He sounded quite bowled over.'

'You – you told him everything?' Fenny's fingernails tore through the chiffon. 'He must have been – surprised.'

'Overwhelmed would be the correct term.'

'Was he angry?'

'Does it matter?' A black eyebrow arched. 'You no longer have to concern yourself with being a compliant lodger in the house of your relations. You have before you the prospect of being the mistress of a large establishment on the island of your husband. That is what you wanted and that is what you have. You should be radiant, although I quite understand that the payment you must make for such benefits is hardly to your liking, and I intend to exact every fraction of that payment regardless of your feelings.'

He paused and his eyes were as hard as lion-coloured stone. 'Your feelings just don't matter to me.'

'Thank you,' she said quietly. 'At least you're honest.'

'One of us has to be, for your veracity isn't to be trusted, is it? You really make a reality of the old adage that the still stream runs faster than the millrace. I look at you, *kyria,* and it's like studying a canvas and wondering what the real picture is like.'

The wine waiter came to the table to discuss with him the various merits of the wines in the restaurant cellar, and Fenny took refuge behind the large menu card. She didn't really have much appetite and gazed without interest at the list of dishes, the entrées and the main courses whose richness made her feel slightly sick.

'Have you decided?' Lion asked her.

'I – I don't fancy anything too exotic. Melon to start with, and then the veal cutlets with new potatoes and French beans.'

'I will have the same,' he told the food waiter, 'except that I shall start with a few slices of smoked ham.'

'Very good, sir.' The waiter collected the menus and looked slightly surprised that a honeymoon couple should dine so simply, especially when the bridegroom was known to be a man of money. As the waiter went away, Lion gave his sardonic smile.

'That man is probably wondering if we have been feeding on love,' he drawled. 'It's ironical, eh, that these people who look at us imagine that today is the happiest of our lives and that we are to be envied?'

'What do you think will be your brothers' reaction?' she just had to ask, recalling the lean, darkly attractive faces of Zonar and Demetre, who were twins and about four years younger than Lion. Demetre had a wife in Greece, but Fenny knew from her cousin that Zonar was a widower, his young wife having died a year after their marriage. That the three brothers were very close, she didn't doubt for an instant, and it was bound to create tension when tomorrow it was she and not Penela who accompanied them to Petaloudes.

The island of butterflies ... and as she sat here with Lion Mavrakis she felt as if some of those butterflies were flying about in her stomach.

'Their surprise will no doubt be considerable,' he said. 'They both admired Penela, so I warn you in advance that they won't be very friendly towards you. They will wonder that I haven't thrown you out on your ear, so the impression I want you to give them is that you love me so desperately that you saw no great harm in taking Penela's place. It will set their minds at rest, for they have very Greek ideas and believe that women should be self-sacrificing. I wouldn't like them to know that you leapt into the lion's den because you saw there a juicy bone in the shape of a rich husband who could provide you with an escape from a routine job and a back bedroom in the house of your relatives.'

'I think it hurts your pride, *kyrie*, that a mere woman should take advantage of you,' she retaliated.

'It infuriates me.' His lips were thin and his eyes were

knives stabbing into her. 'You will do as I tell you with regard to my brothers, for they are closer to my heart than any woman could ever be. I cared for them when they were infants, after our parents were killed by bombs. I raked in the very soil for half-rotten turnips so they wouldn't go completely hungry, and when they grew up I was able to give them the kind of education I couldn't have myself. They have gentler natures than I, *kyria*, and their rough edges have been polished, but like lion cubs they will turn on you if they find out your true nature. Be warned!'

Fenny stared across the table at him and in that moment there was a superb aliveness and arrogance about him, that of a man who with vital determination had got for himself and his brothers a place in the sun, where rotting turnips had no more place on the table. He must have worked like a Trojan and fought like Enyalios to become the formidable man of business that he was, and as Fenny thought of the powerful hardness of his hands when he had touched her, her heart turned over and her bones seemed to run molten.

'I don't have to pretend that I care,' she longed to say to him, without fear or inhibition. 'I took Penela's place because I loved you, desperately.'

As their food was served and their wine was poured, she found herself wondering what love really was and why it struck so suddenly and so deeply. One moment he had been another of Penela's conquests, and the next it was as if her heart had opened and he had stepped right inside. It was a mysterious and alarming sensation ... part of something that gave her no peace ... a torment rather than the romantic experience that the poets wrote about.

She supposed, wistfully, that love was only a sweet, wild madness when it was returned.

'*Stin iyia sou.*' Lion raised his wine glass to her. 'Drink and be merry, for tonight you pay toll on that bridge you crossed into my life.'

Fenny's wine glass trembled in her hand and her lips shook against the brim. Would he be smiling, his eyes ardent and gold, had Penela been here with him? Or was he always a little stern and cruel where women were concerned?

'*Kali oreki,*' she said, letting him know that she knew a smattering of Greek words, carefully memorized for her trip to Crete – a trip she had planned last year, long before Penela had introduced this tall Greek to the members of her family.

'Do you refer to this?' He gestured at the food on his plate. 'Or do you wish me good appetite with regard to your own charms?'

Fenny flushed and set down her wine glass before she upset it and added to the mortification which she already felt. 'Y-you make it very difficult for me to play the role of a – a loving wife,' she said.

'When we're alone there is no need for the masks,' he rejoined. 'Did you know that the Greeks invented the drama played behind a mask? It is part of their belief that human beings are the natural offspring of Janus, with two faces to offer to the world, the mystery being that no one is sure which face is the real one.'

'It's a very cynical attitude.' Fenny ate her melon without really tasting it. 'It implies that no one is really candid and that the world is made up of people playing parts.'

'The more civilized we become the less of ourselves we reveal, and I don't refer to the body but the psyche. Look at you, *kyria*. Your very eyes are a smoke-screen behind which anything could be lurking. Like some husband in a Greek drama, I might be in danger of being poisoned by my smoke-eyed Messalina.'

He laid his knife and fork across his plate. 'Hold out your left hand,' he ordered, and when she did so he touched the great emerald and gave it a slight twist. The gem reversed to one side of the gold band and a tiny cavity was revealed.

'A poisonous powder was kept in that tiny compartment to be tipped into the coffee or wine of the unwanted husband or lover. Ingenious, is it not?'

Fenny gazed at the ring, whose beauty concealed something so sinister. 'Did Penela know about that?' she asked, a little surprised that her cousin hadn't mentioned so fascinating a detail about her engagement ring. Surely a most unusual ring for a man to give to the girl he loved?

He shook his head. 'She asked for an emerald, and I was offered the purchase of that a couple of years ago while on a business trip to Florence. The stone is magnificently carved, but I didn't feel it was necessary to tell Penela that she was wearing a ring reputed to have belonged to Lucrezia Borgia.'

Fenny caught her breath ... the splendid and terrible Borgias, that infamous family devoted to treachery and mysterious death. With a quick twist of his fingers Lion closed the ring again. His smile was narrow, showing the white edge of his teeth.

'Somehow,' he said, 'it seems more appropriate that you should wear the ring, but you have your nerve, you pretty bitch, to wear Penela's emerald.'

Fenny felt the tumult of her nerves at the way his amber eyes raked over her face. No man had ever called her such names, and looked at her with that degree of intensity, as if she were a species of womankind he had never encountered before, arousing in him both antipathy and a strong sense of masculine curiosity.

'I – I only wore it to—' The words half-died in her

throat, and at once he took her up.

'In order to make your act that much more convincing, eh? Let me assure you, my dear, that you are the most consummate little actress I have ever come across, on or off the stage. You are the one who should have taken up a stage career, for I'm certain you could play the role of a *femme fatale* with admirable cunning.'

'Play the role?' she inquired. 'Don't you already think that's what I am – a woman of fatal influence?'

'Yes, that is what you are.' His eyes dwelt on her face with an intensity that was as sharp as a pin driven into a moth. 'And there is always a certain fascination in the company of the devil's daughter.'

'I can tell by the way you say such things that you really mean to be insulting.' It hurt abominably to be thought so little of by the only man in the world who mattered to her. Men until now had made as much impression on her as their names written on water, but Lion had a forthright honesty that was like a diamond cutting into glass. It cut into her and she had to endure the pain, but that didn't mean that she had to be spiritless. He expected a fight and he knew how to get under her skin, igniting a spark each time he looked at her ... each time he let her know with brutal frankness that he was utterly scornful of the trick she had played on him.

'Insults are always more sincere than flattery,' he told her. 'Mmm, this is excellent veal, don't you think?'

'Very nice,' she agreed, but she ate her cutlets and French beans without really tasting them. She was wondering what Penela's reaction would be when she heard from Uncle Dominic ... no, it wouldn't be necessary for Penela's father to be in touch with her about Lion's marriage. Penela would scan the newspapers in order to find out how he had taken it when she failed to turn up at the church, but instead of reading that Lion Mavrakis had been jilted she would read that he had been married!

Fenny knew her cousin... she would be infuriated that, to all appearances, he had turned so casually to another bride. Who could possibly believe that he had gone through the ceremony in total unawareness that the girl at his side was not Penela?

It was almost as if he had never really known her cousin... or was it true what he said, that no woman held his heart, or ever could slip through its iron doors that he seemed to keep closed on everyone but the twin brothers he had reared from infancy?

Fenny gave him a quick look, but his face was impassive as a Greek mask. He could have felt many things, but she couldn't see in him a trace of heartache. No, she thought, too much had happened to him, from his deprived boyhood to his attainment of wealth and an island of his own, for a mere creature of bright hair and a willowy body to inflict any abiding pain.

It was his pride that was hurt, and he would see to it that she paid the price.

When the dessert trolley came to the table, he said to her in his silkiest tone of voice: 'Sweets for the sweet, eh? Come, you must have some of that delicious-looking flan, and some of those berries in syrup, and how about a piece of that layered cake? After all, you didn't have any of your own wedding cake, did you, my dear?'

'I – I couldn't eat another thing,' she said. 'I really don't want any dessert—'

'Ah, but I insist, *kyria*. Once those delectables are on your plate, you will wolf them down. Now is your chance to taste the good things of life – yes, waiter, my wife will have a sweet.'

'Perhaps Madame would like the nectarines, sir?' The waiter glanced at Fenny. 'We light them with brandy and then add cream. It gives them a most subtle flavour.'

'Yes, we'll have those,' Lion said, a slight curl to his lips as he looked at Fenny. 'A special day in our lives calls for a special treat. Make the brandy the best you have, and add a couple of those large pears called white bells.'

The ritual proceeded while Fenny sat there white-faced, feeling sure that Lion was forcing her to be as physically sick as she made him feel, sitting opposite to him in the dress chosen by Penela, wearing the pearls, he had selected for his first night gift to his bride. He had chosen Penela, whether he loved her or not.

Fenny he hadn't chosen and he was letting her know it with every subtle nuance of his gravelly Greek voice; every glance he gave her, that brow *diable* lifting away from the amber eyes as hard as stones in the strong face.

The brandy flared with a devilish blue light as the flame was added to the cognac-smothered fruit, and Fenny watched as if mesmerized as the pale cream extinguished the fire. The waiter bowed and left the table, and Fenny picked up her fork and spoon with unsteady hands.

'Mmm, the flavour is certainly subtle,' Lion murmured. 'Come, eat your fruit and cream, and stop pretending that you have the appetite of the innocent birds.'

'You are being cruel,' she gasped. 'Stop it!'

'Don't you presume to give orders to me.' His eyes flashed at her and she caught a frightening glimpse of the primitive Greek under the façade of a good suit and the modern grooming of his black hair. In an instant he became a Greek who had known the underworld, for no man climbed high without having known the depths, and it was there in Lion's eyes that he had the instincts of the jungle in his fierce veins. There in that lamplit restaurant he suddenly looked as ruthless as a tiger with its victim.

'I am being myself, *kyria*.' His voice grated the words.

'I am just a hard, self-made Greek with no illusions about anyone, and you will have to learn that where my wife is concerned my word is law.'

'And so I must stuff myself with brandied fruit whether I want it or not?'

'And I must be the husband of a little fake, whether I want it or not!'

'You have no pity at all?' she asked.

'Not an atom where you are concerned. Now eat, or we shall be late for the theatre.'

And he sat there like an inquisitor until Fenny had consumed most of the brandied nectarine and the pear that was exactly the shape of a bell. She thought of the strange Byzantine music of the bells of the Greek church, and the rice and rose petals falling against the long lacy skirts of the wedding dress. She had been put into a gleaming black car with a Greek woman, a relative of Demetre's wife, who hadn't really known Fenny from Eve, excitedly squeezing her cold hand as they drove away from the church ... promising her that she had a real man *to love her*.

There had not been anyone for years to really care about Fenny, but she had grown used to the loneliness of the feeling. But nothing had ever prepared her for the cold hatred that seemed to strike into her very bones as Lion took her by the elbow and led her from the restaurant to the street, where a car waited to take them to the Aldwych.

They drove there in silence and when Fenny stepped from the car into the streaming lights the cloak around her glimmered like the scales of a fish, and there was an air of Ophelia about her as with outward, lethal charm her tall husband escorted her down the aisle to their seats.

The cloak rustled as she sat down ... people glanced

and saw a face they would never have taken for a bride's.

Lion leaned down to her and his breath struck warm against her ear. ' "I am very proud, revengeful, ambitious ..." ' he murmured, quoting the Prince of Denmark. 'It is too late, my dear, for you to get to a nunnery!'

Fenny strove not to look at him, afraid of his eyes and what they did to her nerves. The lights of the theatre began to dim and the great curtain to rise. There were the ramparts of the castle ... there the setting for the wonderful sound and exciting fury of Shakespeare.

It was during the second interval that a kind of madness came over Fenny, caught perhaps from Ophelia in her tragic bid to win the love of Hamlet.

She excused herself from Lion, murmuring a wish to visit the powder-room. But when she reached the foyer she escaped through the small crowd of people smoking and discussing the play and made her way out of the swing doors of the theatre. Catching her cloak about her slim figure, she hastened along the lamplit pavement, walking down towards the Strand, her face as pale as ice in the glare of car lights and the amber street lamps. She was running from Lion, perhaps with no real hope in her heart that she would escape him, but for now ... for a while she was free of that 'face without a heart'.

She crossed the road and made for the steps that led down to the Embankment. The smell of the river came to her, pulling her like Ophelia to the cool dark water flowing beneath the stone balustrade of the bridge.

The night around her and the glimmering lights on the water created a sense of transient peace, the first she had known all day. The breeze wafted against her face and lazily moved a soft strand of her hair ... there was a certain beauty to this old, unchanging part of London and at any other time Fenny would have surrendered herself to it. But when she looked down into the water, she saw there a pair of glittering eyes. In the distant rumble of traffic she heard the anger in a deep voice. In the hard stone beneath her fingers she felt the coldness of Lion's touch.

Sudden tears trembled in Fenny's eyes ... much of this was Penela's fault, yet she escaped censure and the whip fell on her own shoulders. When they were at school together Penela had always bluffed her way out of a scrape, while Fenny's innate honesty had brought her face to face with retribution.

Little daggers of gold danced on the river, and Fenny felt in every nerve of her body the approach of Lion before he came and stood over her.

'Full of surprises, aren't you?' he said. 'Were you planning to follow the example of Hamlet's *amour tragique*?'

'I'm not a coward,' she replied. 'I just had to get away by myself for a few minutes. You didn't have to follow me – I'd have come back to the theatre.'

'Of course,' he said, and in the misty amber lighting his face was stamped with irony. 'You have no legal part of my possessions until you become my wife in more than name.'

'I never wanted your possessions,' she denied. 'I never gave them a thought.'

'My dear, don't protest that you do me the honour of wanting me!' He gave a low, sarcastic laugh. 'When I touch you, you go as tense as a poker. I can actually feel you steeling yourself to endure my rough hands upon your smooth skin. I hope you will find that Petaloudes is sufficient compensation for the sacrifice you must make of yourself – for that you must do, *kyria,* biology being the master of us all. You will pay me back with a son, and I don't much care if you are willing or not. The brides of Sparta were usually taken by force.'

Fenny, who had never indulged in the casual flirtations and encounters so dear to modern-minded girls like Penela, was in every sense of the word a chaste person. She wasn't afraid of Lion's passion; what shook her heart was that he would treat her as if she were no better than any pick-up along the Strand, where the car stood waiting for them.

She slipped inside with a silken rustle of the long cloak, and as he joined her, his hard body brushed against her, and when she gave an involuntary shiver, she heard him give that low, unamused laugh.

' "Frailty, thy name is woman!" ' he mocked. 'It has been said that a certain greatly gifted actor always quoted that line with an air of surprise – as well he might!'

'You are very cynical about women, *kyrie*.' Although the glass partition was lowered between them and the driver of the limousine, she spoke in a low voice. She was, in fact, beginning to feel rather frail after a day of trauma, and she couldn't help but wonder what Lion would do if she suddenly allowed her tired head to sink against his broad shoulder. Would he push her away from him, or kiss her as a man kissed a bought woman?

Either reaction would be unbearable and so she sat there, to all outward appearance cool, proud and distant.

'A man can only judge women by those he has known, *kyria*. When I was a much younger man I had no time to give to them, for I was always too busy. It was enough to have the casual pleasure of a lady of the night, but I never thought seriously of marriage until in Athens last summer I met your cousin. Well, she has turned out fickle, and the fates have tricked me into marriage with you. If I am cynical who can blame me? But as I am also Greek I must make of a bad bargain a reward of some sort. You haven't the instant attraction of your cousin, but you know how to wear her clothes and you have an air of chastity that intrigues even a man who knows it to be false. As much of a cloak as this silky garment you hug about your slim-hipped body.'

His glance was like a blade, from her brow to her lips, from her bosom to her hips. 'You aren't built for prodigious breeding, but I want only the one child of you and the chances are good that it will be a son. My parents had only sons, and Zonar's wife bore him a boy child before she died.'

'I had no idea your brother Zonar was a father.' Fenny looked surprised, and realized anew how little she really knew about Lion and his family. 'He looks – oh, I don't know.'

'Carefree, eh? A man who flirts and treats life as if it were going to end in the morning. It's a mask! He, unlike Demetre and myself, was lucky in love – until that infamous lorry ran into their car and Mercedes was so badly injured that she gave birth on the side of the road where the crash occurred, dying before the ambulance could reach the hospital.'

'The child lived?' Fenny looked at her husband with a sincere compassion in her eyes. He stared back at her with cold eyes, and said in a cutting voice:

'Spare me your big-eyed play-acting. What does it matter to you, that a Mavrakis should suffer? You are no chosen member of my family. You invaded our privacy, so keep your honeyed sympathy for yourself; for the day when I keep your baby and throw you out of my life. I shall do it, and you will have to endure the pain of having a child who will never run to you and call you mother.'

'Y-you'll be that cruel?' she asked, a hand at her throat to hold back the scream that was conceived in her before the child he would force her to have. Everything about him threatened force ... the dark sternness of his face, the hard width of his shoulders, the way his work-hardened fingers scraped the silk of her cloak.

'Retribution is never tender,' he said. 'A Greek expects neither mercy nor love of life, but he works hard in order to have a son to whom he can give, hopefully, a better life. Yes, Zonar's child is alive and well, and in the care of a nurse at the *kastello*. I might have made Alekos my heir, but in the circumstances I shall make use of you and have an heir of my own body.'

And as he spoke Lion leaned close to her, his brief smile at its most terrifying. 'I am beginning to feel quite enthusiastic about the procedure. Did you know that in Greek the word enthusiasm means that a person is possessed by a god?'

'Not a devil?' she whispered, feeling all the dark force of him as he gazed down at her with strange fires burning in his eyes. She sensed again that pagan streak in him ... that promise of a ruthlessness that no amount of pleading would soften or dent. He would take her as the ancient gods took their sacrifices from the stone altars ... as the men of Sparta their brides in the dark, unknowing, uncaring if they had fair faces and kind hearts.

A woman would do the one thing that a man couldn't ... she could be made to bear a child.

'The devil has been at work today, so why not tonight?' he murmured. 'It could be a heaven and a hell of a wedding night.'

As he spoke the car came to a standstill at the entrance of the Parkway Towers. They entered through the swing doors and crossed the foyer to the desk, where Lion collected their key from the night clerk. He gave them both that slightly salacious smile of the young male who knew them to be honeymooners.

'Goodnight, sir – madam.' He emphasized the words, and Fenny didn't dare to look at Lion as they entered the lift that swept them to the penthouse floor. Everything was very quiet, for it was late and the lights had been dimmed in the hall of their suite. The turning of the key in the lock played on Fenny's strung nerves, and when they entered the sitting-room she tensed at the firm closing of the door, shutting them in together.

'Do you fancy a nightcap?' he asked, throwing off his topcoat and approaching the bar. 'I am going to have a vodka gimlet – very good for the nerves.'

'Why, are you nervous?' she felt compelled to say.

'Not in the least, but you are, aren't you? You would like to be one of those wives who pleads a headache and escapes the amorous attentions of a fond husband. I don't care a curse what aches you have, whether they are connected with the heart or the head.'

Bottles clinked and the two pale spirits were joined in a pair of glasses. Fenny dropped her cloak to the couch and accepted one of the glasses. She had never tasted vodka, but if it would help to steady her racing pulse then she wouldn't care if it tasted like vinegar. She swallowed quickly and felt the strong spirit in her throat, almost making her gag until she forced it down.

'It strikes me as odd that you haven't – or so it would appear – the sophistication of Penela.' He watched her and the way she took another swallow at her drink, as if it were a medicine. 'I think I must presume that you know all the tricks of the game you have played on me, and if you hope to soften my heart with your little acts of false piety and virtue, then it's a waste of effort. Save your strength, my dear.'

She flushed at the way he looked and spoke, his eyes travelling over her as if she were some kind of ornament on the side table.

Then he said to her, almost insolently: 'It's about time for bed, so you might as well go to your room. Get ready for me – I shall join you in a very short while.'

Fenny stared back at him, petrified by the implication in his words.

'Well, you married me, didn't you?' he drawled.

'Yes—'

'Then what are you waiting for? You were anxious enough to dress yourself in your cousin's wedding gown, and now is the time for you to get ready for our wedding night.'

'You can't mean that—' They were foolish words, but they wouldn't be held back. Fenny knew all too well that Lion meant everything he said to her.

He quirked an eyebrow. 'I never waste breath on unessential remarks, and I believe you know it. Penela's nightwear should fit you, but if it doesn't, then I shan't complain—'

'Lion, please!' It was the last desperate cry of the condemned, and it broke from Fenny, cracking the pride she had sworn to keep intact.

'My dear, you can sound quite moving, but you should have considered the consequences of your action this morning – as the day wanes the night falls – as the night passes the dawn arrives. There is no escape from life and death, and the debts we incur. Go to your room!'

And without looking at him again she went, dragging the silk cloak at her heels.

In the quiet luxury of her lamplit bedroom Fenny disrobed for bed, lost in thought as she moved about on the soft carpet, entering the bathroom to wash and brush her teeth, and re-entering to put on the nightdress of soft apricot silk trimmed with *point de rose* lace.

The coming confrontation with Lion filled her with a strange mixture of feelings. There were wild and lawless forces in him ... her unloving husband. The pearly paleness of her skin, the loosened gold of her hair, the trembling shadows of her lashes wouldn't move him to tenderness, only to a desire that a virile man might feel for a woman who actually belonged to him.

The mirror reflected back her nubile image ... that face and body were the possessions of Lion Mavrakis and very soon now he would come and claim them ... if only it might be in love ... her breast lifted on a sigh and she saw the sadness in her smoky eyes, and the shadow of desperation. He would enslave her but never love her, and slowly she turned to gaze at the low, wide bed covered by gold-tawny silk.

Hers would, indeed, be a heaven and a hell of a wedding night.

She was standing by the windows, looking out upon the stars that seemed to hang low above the Towers, when she caught the sound of the bedroom door being opened. With her heart racing Fenny went on standing there, feeling the clamour of her pulses as he trod silently across the carpet and with a supple, animal movement tilted back her head until her hair streamed over his fingers and her neck felt stretched. She was made helpless, aware that she would wrench her neck muscles if she tried to break from his grip. She quivered as his free hand caressed her, and sensations never felt before ran like fire through her blood, and trembled over her skin in the chemise nightdress of fine silk, leaving her shoulders white and bare under his touch. It was nothing but another silken veil, flowing down over her slenderness.

His hand moved up under her hair and his fingers clasped her neck. 'One of the most vulnerable and yet most erotic items of a woman's anatomy is the nape of her neck,' he murmured, and in the tumult and wildness of that moment Fenny could almost have believed there had been a caressing inflection in his voice, but then he swung her around and she saw his face and any hope of tenderness was crushed by the inflexibility of his features above the black silk robe open against his brown chest. In the lamplight there was a barbaric quality to his facial bones, his amber eyes, and thick black hair.

Those eyes moved over her, heavy-lidded, and dwelt on a curling tendril of hair that clung golden to the side of her neck. 'Your skin has the fine pallor of the lotus, my dear. How innocent you look – a man might almost be fooled into thinking you had led the life of a cloistered nun.'

With these words he brought her close to his bare chest in a single, almost voluptuous movement of his strong hands. The firm masculinity of him was pressed to her and she closed her eyes as she felt his lips on her bare skin. She was heart-shaken by the stabs of love and fear going through her.

'How can you do this – you don't love me!' The words broke achingly from her, for she knew that the feel of her was firing him to a desire that was utterly sensuous and physical, without a shadow of love in his eyes or upon his lips.

'What has loving you to do with – this?' He gave a wicked threat of a laugh and his fingers traced the fine bones under her soft young skin. 'You shall be my *robija* – my slave of a thousand nights, and then *adio!*'

He held her a moment away from him and what he felt was showing nakedly in his eyes. She had never seen that kind of look before, making his eyes tiger-gold in his dark face; making a pulse beat madly beside his lips.

Fenny threw out a hand as if to ward him off. 'Please—'

' "Who wants forgiveness must first knock at the door and wait for the devil to answer." ' He spoke mockingly and held her helpless between his hands, his warmth penetrating through the apricot silk.

'It would be like knocking on stone,' she gasped.

'Assuredly.' He caught her hand and held it to his chest. 'Stone.'

But stone wasn't warm and tanned, with a crisp feel of hair crossing his heart.

'You are acting just like a virgin with her first man,' he taunted.

'Y-you know that I am—'

'Not yet I know it, *melle mou.*' He swung her up into his arms and with his catlike walk he made for the bed and as he laid her down her hair was flung like silk across her face, in which before she could move his fingers were tangled. She saw his nostrils quiver as he caught the scent of her hair and her skin, and despite her terror she knew herself seduced by his touch, and by the look he had of a man who wouldn't spare her until dawn came creeping through the windows.

As he put out the lamp, he gave that wickedly soft laugh and she heard the rustle of silk as he threw off his robe. 'All cats feel soft in the dark – and they can all be made to purr,' he said.

CHAPTER THREE

THE morning sunlight played over tumbled gold hair against the silk pillows and moved its way across Fenny's eyelids. In a while she stirred and her eyes opened to a strange room with luxurious fittings; she lay there idly and it was several seconds before she felt the impact of where she was, and with a gasp she sat upright, clutching the tawny-gold bedcover around her.

Now she remembered everything ... no longer was she the naïve girl of yesterday, for there wasn't an inch of her, not a toe or a nerve which had not felt the intimacy of Lion's lips.

He had possessed her from her golden hair to the soles of her feet, and her body still tingled from those endless hours in his arms ... he had been cruel at times, uncaring that she was innocent, taunting her even as he made her yield to him.

There in the night nothing had mattered except that she loved him, yet even so she had not surrendered without a fight, and she knew that if he had loved anything at all about her, he had loved it that she fought with him ... fought until he made her surrender.

She had been totally conquered in the darkness, but now it was daytime and she must face him and endure the knowledge that the pleasure he had found with her had nothing to do with love. Not once had he whispered a tender word ... he had found her body pleasing and that was all. She might have been a slave girl with her pasha, for that was how she had felt in his strong arms, feeling the hard, wild passion of a man she loved but hardly knew.

She was sitting there, lost in her thoughts, when the bedroom door abruptly opened and Lion strode in upon her, dark and virile in a white polo shirt and immaculate dark trousers. A wave of confusion swept over Fenny, and she clasped the bedcovers closely about her, feeling as if a flame ran over her skin instead of a pair of masculine eyes.

'*Kalimera*,' he greeted her, and she saw the devilish amusement curling about his lips that she should attempt to hide herself from his eyes. He came and stood at the bedside and he flicked a look from her face to the crumpled pillowcase beside her. Then he casually let fall an object that had a burning lustre in the morning sun.

'The gift of virginity must always be rewarded if the gods are to be appeased,' he said. '*Evkaristo, mou.*'

Fenny stared at the object, and there ran wildly through her veins the awareness that she was being paid for last night just like any harem creature, and there was a dark-skinned, barbaric quality to Lion that whispered of old Turkish harems and the occupation of Greece long ago of those fierce lovers of women.

'Look at it,' he ordered. 'You may find pleasure in it.'

'As you found your pleasure when you discovered that I had never been used before?' she asked, and her eyes were stormy as she looked at him, so very male and sure of himself; so vitalized by a wedding night which had lingered on into the pallor of the dawn.

'It quite shook me,' he admitted, leaning down to her with an arm stretched to the back of the bed, 'to find you so immaculate in body even if you had such a deceitful mind. Did I hurt you, *kyria*?'

'What of it?' A deep flush came into her cheeks. 'That was what you wanted, *kyrie*, to hurt me.'

'All the same—' His dark hand slipped to her bare

shoulder. 'I am not quite an animal, but a man's anger, and a man's passion, can overcome his better side. You have very white skin and it must easily bruise.'

His touch on her skin sent right through Fenny those incredible sensations that met like sparks in the pit of her stomach. 'Don't do that – don't touch me this morning,' she whispered.

His fingers tightened a moment and then withdrew. 'Look at your gift. I am sure it will compensate in some measure.'

She allowed her fingers to pick up the golden bracelet, in a charming design of berries and flowers and tiny female heads. It was obviously Grecian and probably a rare antique.

'That is a design sacred to Aphrodite,' he told her. 'The filigree work is excellent, and quite attractive, don't you think?'

'Very pretty,' she said. 'Very appropriate for your slave girl.'

'So long as you know what you are. Would you like breakfast up here on the terrace of the suite, or down in the restaurant?'

'Up here on the terrace would be nice,' she said, tensing as he took her wrist and clasped the bracelet about it, his eyes watching her through his black lashes as she pressed the coverlet to her with her other hand.

'My brothers will be calling for us soon after we have breakfasted.' His fingers pressed against her wristbone.

'You remember what I told you?'

'Yes, *kyrie*. I must act the besotted bride and convince them that the loss of Penela as a sister-in-law is not too much of a calamity. I must, if possible, look a picture of wifely reserve and devotion.'

'You will also learn to use my name – as you used it last night.'

'Did I?' She was confused all over again. Heaven help her, she could have said anything to him during those hours alone with him, high above the world, lost to everything but the touch and feel of the lithe, iron-hard body of a man who had spent his life in the sun and seas of Greece, and was steeped in the law of male dominance.

Nothing had mattered then ... but now she burned in case she had said something that gave away her heart to him.

'You will never know, will you?' he taunted her softly. 'Do you need a valet to help you bathe?'

'Indeed I don't,' she gasped, tingling at the very thought.

'Strange enigma, aren't you?' He caught her by the chin and held her face to the sunlight, a merciless glint in his raking eyes. 'You know less than half of what Penela knows about men, yet you carry off a deception that fooled even your uncle. You must have been desperate to get rich quickly and I hope that each payment will not be too unbearable for you. Last night you fought like a little demon, until I had you subdued.'

'Do you have to remind me of – last night?' Fenny had to cling to her pride, for it was all she had left. 'You're very much stronger than me – I had to give in to you whether I wanted to or not.'

'Perhaps so.' His smile was sardonic. 'It was in all ways an unexpected wedding night, and while you are mine you will be in every sense of the word my exclusive property – the wife of a Greek doesn't look at other men unless she wants a beating. We have a saying, beat your woman as you beat your sheepskin rug.'

'How charming!'

'Greeks don't pretend to have the specious charm of other men. What we say, we mean. What we do, we do thoroughly.'

'I'm convinced of that,' she said feelingly.

He laughed, a gravelly sound in his brown throat. 'I will go into the sitting-room and order our breakfast. Don't keep me waiting.'

'No, pasha.'

'What – what was that you said?' He leaned down to her again, his eyes stabbing their gold at her.

'You heard me.' She drew away from him, still so very unsure of him.

'Merciful heaven, there is no need for that look in your eyes. You may have your own name for me, if you wish, but not in front of other people, I beg of you! Least of all my brothers!'

He left her with long strides, closing the door in that firm way behind him, as if shutting away what belonged to him – his exclusive property in the slim shape of a girl who had married him, so he thought, for his hard-earned wealth and his private island.

Fenny skipped out of bed and made for the bathroom, where she turned on the shower and stood for long moments under the invigorating lash of the water, soaping her body that seemed more sentient, and she noticed that despite her struggles with Lion he had hardly marked her with his powerful yet knowing hands.

How many women had there been in his life? He was in his late thirties, and his vigour excluded the thought that he had ever lived like a monk.

Had he made love to Penela? This was the one notion that Fenny could hardly bear to face, and the probability was that he had held her cousin in his arms as he had held her last night. Hadn't he said that she knew less than half of what Penela knew about men! A remark that surely seemed to indicate an intimate knowledge of her cousin?

A sensation of jealousy stabbed through Fenny. Had he

compared them in his mind and found her own inexperience both prudish and amusing? She would never really know, for she was only a possession to him, to be enjoyed or set aside, as the mood took him.

Briskly she rubbed down with a bath-towel, trying to wipe away her thoughts as she wiped away the water. On her return to the bedroom she clad herself in the spun-silk lingerie that Penela had bought with Lion's money, and selected for the journey to Greece a dusty-pink skirt in soft gloving leather, and a paler pink shirt with a wide-open collar. There were smart dapple-kid shoes to go with the outfit, and once again she had to fit them with the cardboard inners so they wouldn't fall off her feet.

As she brushed her hair it crackled with life in the morning sunlight and had a sheen to it that made her stare into the mirror. Yesterday's terror had left her eyes; it was only inside that she still felt that quickening of fear and fascination at the mere thought of being part of Lion Mavrakis.

She was a part of him and nothing could alter that. He was the first and only man who had ever known her, in that Biblical term of those days when it was more of a sin for men to make love to women outside the bonds of marriage.

She and Lion were bonded together, and that possession would continue for as long as she remained childless.

Fenny loved him, even more than yesterday, and she didn't dare to get pregnant. If she bore Lion a son, then he would keep his Grecian word and put her away from him. It was that torturing thought that brought the terror back into her smoky eyes, and she had to wait several seconds before she felt calm enough to join her husband on the terrace of the penthouse suite.

It was high above the busy streets of London and the

green belt of trees and parkland. He was at the ironwork table reading the morning paper and he gave her a brief glance as she walked to the parapet and gazed downwards at the London she would be leaving in so short a time, bound for an island in the Aegean Sea ... that wondrous sea which had given birth to Aphrodite of the foam ... goddess of love.

Fenny glanced at the gold bracelet which Lion had given her to appease his pagan gods, and its very quaintness appealed to her far more than the sophisticated pearls of last night.

'We haven't a great deal of time, Fenella.' He spoke her name for the very first time, saying it firmly but with no intonation to quicken her heart. 'You had better eat some food, for the flight to Greece will take some hours, and there will be only sandwiches and coffee to break the fast. I want to get to Petaloudes on a matter of business.'

'Don't you ever stop working?' she asked him, as she sat down and poured herself a cup of tea.

'Not if I can help it,' he replied, lifting the cover of the bacon dish and putting a couple of slices on her plate, adding scambled egg and kidneys. 'There, that should invigorate you.'

'Thank you,' she said, and found herself extremely hungry. Lion had already eaten, and a brief glance showed her that he was deep in the financial section of his newspaper. On his wrist there was a black-strapped watch with the dark hairs of his wrist curling against the leather, and she felt a quiver of sheerest sensuality run completely through her. Those hands had held her, subdued her, and caressed every inch of her. She felt a stab of remembered emotion, shocking in its intensity.

There was nothing basically gentle about love ... it really was the most primitive of human experiences.

Fenny tried not to stare at this man who made her feel

this way ... that she loved him to her very bones was undeniable. She felt as if his touch had left upon every bit of her the powerful, unforgettable imprint of his personality.

She felt a disturbing tumult of her pulses as he glanced up and looked directly into her eyes, catching and holding her gaze before she could transfer it to her marmalade and toast.

'I am glad to see you are in good appetite, *kyria*. Perhaps it's the morning air, eh?'

She flushed slightly and his eyes narrowed as they took in her silky hair and skin. 'Strange that I ever thought you insignificant,' he said, and his lips twisted in a slight smile. 'When I used to see you at your uncle's house I hardly noticed you – what is it, your hair? You used to wear it differently, perhaps? At the nape of your neck?'

She nodded. 'When you work in an office, hair worn loose can be a bother when you have to keep bending over a typewriter. I got into the habit of wearing my hair that way.'

'And no doubt in the habit of not competing with your cousin,' he drawled. 'While you remain with me, I would prefer you to keep your hair in the style you have it right now. I want you to be admired, and there is a strange, singular beauty to your eyes. But be warned, other men may look, but they will not touch!'

'As if I'd want them to touch me!' She looked indignant, and underneath she felt shaken by his comment on her looks. She knew that as a Greek he merely wished to take pride in what his money had bought, but all the same – from him it was like a bunch of roses!

'Of course, my dear. I had forgotten that you had a disinclination to be touched, and no doubt you'd prefer it if I found you unappealing in that way. Unfortunately for you I find your slim body rather delightful – come, there is no need to blush. You must have realized last night that I wasn't exactly disappointed. I had pleasure of you, so you can eat that good food with a clear conscience and wear those pretty clothes in the happy knowledge that you have earned them.'

'Oh, Lion—'

'That is exactly how you said it last night, *melle mou*. Keep on saying my name like that and my brothers will approve of you.'

'You – you can be as hurtful as a lion,' she gasped.

'Yes, it's as well that you never forget that I can. Fenella in the lion's den, eh? Do you hope to charm me into eating out of your hand?'

'I could never hope to live that long,' she rejoined.

'Long enough to give me what I want.' He reached for a white peach and broke it open, expelling the stone and handing her one of the halves. The juice ran from his fingers to hers, and as always there seemed a strange significance in all that he did. It was the Greek in him, those links with all that was mythical and pagan. Rites of love, magic and war. Great stones of sacrifice in the burning sun. The silver olive tree, and the fertile fig, from the harsh soil of his ancient land.

Fenny bit into the flesh of the peach ... his white teeth did the same.

They were still sitting in the sun on the terrace when the buzzer was pressed beside the door of the suite. Fenny felt an immediate tension, and when Lion rose to his feet she knew that he was about to let his brothers into the sitting-room. She nerved herself, and then followed him. There was no escape from these men; they had to be faced in the lonely knowledge that she hadn't Lion's love to back her up.

He opened the main door, and immediately dark hands were grasping broad shoulders and it was as if the three of them had been apart for a month instead of a night.

Greeks, from their black hair to their resilient feet, with a powerful family attachment that could exclude the stranger completely, if they so willed it.

'The newly married man,' laughed Zonar. 'Head of the house and only now a husband! How goes it, brother?'

'*Endaxi*,' he rejoined the deep voice with its older tones, those in which authority were mingled with an indulgence never applied to Fenny. She knew the authority well enough but not the affection.

The brothers strolled into the room, overpowering Fenny with their height and their darkness. They were alike but not strikingly so, and they both had smoother looks than Lion. They were very good-looking, but their impact was less daunting, and they had dark brown eyes instead of the dusky-gold that made the glance of the eldest brother so meaningful.

The two sets of dark eyes were fixed upon her. 'You look different.' It was Demetre who spoke first. 'A little less – or is it more—?'

'It's a different girl.' Zonar swept his eyes over her shining hair like a bell of corn. 'The quiet, beautiful one!'

Fenny stood there, with no defence against the brothers and their opinion of her. They had intensely male eyes that appraised her from head to toe, and she heard Lion flick his lighter at a cheroot, almost lazily unconcerned by her feeling of being on trial, his brothers her judge and jury.

'What the devil has gone wrong?' Demetre looked puzzled and angry.

'Or right?' Zonar stared at Fenny, and now she noticed that he looked different from his twin because a certain suffering had stamped lines into his face and made him look more like Lion. He stepped towards her and a smile

71

came into his eyes. 'May I kiss your hand and welcome you to our family?'

Fenny had no time to protest or agree, for Zonar impulsively took her ringed hand and carried it to his lips. 'You are very beautiful – golden hair and such flawless skin, so rare in this day and age when the cosmetician can do so many things to embellish the female.'

At the touch of Zonar's lips on her hand, Fenny instantly realized that a rather dangerous thing had happened; she felt that Zonar Mavrakis was attracted to her, and she hastily pulled free her fingers from his.

'Lion, you are a lucky man,' he said.

'Am I?' The lean, hard face was wreathed in cheroot smoke; the amber eyes partly hooded and unreadable.

'But of course, brother. How many men drop a silver piece and pick up a charm of gold?'

'I am glad you are so smitten by my bride.' A flicker of gold eyes went across Fenny's face. 'She was concerned that my brothers approve of her.'

'Approve?' Demetre gave his older brother an astounded look. 'Are we really to accept this girl in place of the one to whom you were officially engaged? She is an impostor—'

'No,' Lion corrected him. 'She and I were married in church yesterday morning, and last night we became man and wife. There is no more to be said!'

'There are many things to be said,' Demetre protested. 'These things just don't happen—'

'It would seem, Metre, that they do happen – even to Greeks.' Lion's smile was the very essence of irony. 'But a woman is a woman when all is said and done, and this one will suffice for my needs. A pleasing face at the dinner table; a little solace at the end of the day.'

It was then that Fenny felt she had to leave the Mavrakis family to work this out among themselves, and acting upon instinct she moved across the room to Lion and stood almost upon the points of her toes in order to reach his hard, creviced cheek with her lips. 'I must see that the luggage is ready,' she said. 'I know that you want to get away.'

'Quite so, Fenella,' He shot a glance at Demetre. 'You see how obedient she is?'

'Tamed to your hand – already?' queried Zonar. He followed her to the door which she approached and opened it for her. He watched as she entered the bedroom she had shared with Lion, and she knew that his dark eyes dwelt upon the bed before she closed the door behind her.

Fenny stood very still a moment, her palms pressed to her hot face. What an incredible situation it was ... Demetre obviously disapproved of her, while Zonar had taken a fancy to her. Greeks! They did nothing by half measures! Why couldn't they be as casually disinterested as an Englishman would have been in the marriage of a brother?

She pressed her fingers against her scalp, disarranging her hair. But it had to be faced that Lion was no ordinary brother. He had slaved and possibly gone without in order that his twin brothers should survive the harsh winters at the end of the war. He had used all his strength and acumen in order to make life good for them ... there wasn't a fractional doubt in Fenny's mind that both brothers adored him and wanted him to be happy with the right woman.

In Demetre's opinion Penela wasn't easily replaced by someone else, for she had been the woman chosen by Lion to be his wife. Zonar, on the other hand, had looked at Fenny and said instantly: 'It's the quiet, beautiful one!'

Beautiful? Fenny walked to the mirror and gave herself a long, objective look. Her looks were extremely fair and

73

English, and it was that about her which probably appealed to the young Greek who since the tragic loss of his wife had probably played around with women in order to try and forget his unhappiness.

But it must be understood by him that he couldn't play around with her. She was Lion's wife ... his possession, and she felt sure there would be hell to pay if she ever allowed Zonar to lay his hands upon her. It wasn't only accursed by Greeks that a man should covet his brother's wife, it just wasn't in Lion's nature to share his woman with anyone. She was *his*, to kiss or beat ... to hold or discard.

Life with him seemed to pull her into deep waters whichever way she looked.

She took up a comb and ran it through her hair until the bell of gold was smooth again. Then she turned to the bed and folded her night things into the smaller of the three pigskin cases ... her heart thumped and for the first time she noticed the monogram upon them. A lion giving out with a silent roar, and the initials PM.

Nothing was hers! Not the man, or the clothes, or that Grecian island in the sun.

Demetre had called her an impostor, and it was true! She had no right to be here, yet she had nowhere else to go. Uncle Dominic would refuse to know her after the way she had behaved, daring to step into his darling Penela's shoes ... which in every sense of the word were proving too big for her!

The bedroom door swept open and Lion appeared. 'The porter is here to take down the luggage,' he said. 'Are you ready?'

'Yes.' She picked up the jacket that matched her skirt, and took up the handbag that matched the over-large shoes. For a moment she felt an hysterical urge to laugh ... but it was laughter that would have ended in tears if she had given way to it.

'All ready,' she said, and walked from the room in which she had lost her innocence to Lion, learning heartache and rapture from a master of both.

She and the brothers drove in one of those long dark limousines to the helipad on the outskirts of London. It stood there awaiting them, the big scarlet cage of steel and glass that was the private helicopter in which Lion flew back and forth from his island to his places of business.

As they walked towards it, she and the three tall men, it seemed to grow larger until its gleaming rotors were way above her head. The luggage was stowed aboard, and she climbed the steel steps into the big cabin with its four passenger seats. The pilot was already seated at the controls, and she gave Zonar a brief, grateful smile as he settled her near the curving window. 'Comfortable?' he murmured.

She nodded, and saw his lips quirk as he went to his seat beside Demetre, who was still looking at her as if he found her hard to believe in. He was probably more introspective than Zonar, and therefore deeply shocked by what she had done. She must seem to him quite shameless, and his attitude would probably be his wife's as well. Fenny's hands nervously clenched the handbag on her lap ... oh lord, how could she know if she was flying off to Hades or heaven?

'Nervous?' Lion had taken the seat beside her. 'You have never flown in a chopper before?'

She shook her head and wished he would hold her hand as the whirling blades of the machine lifted it clear into the air, so that it swung out over the silvery ribbon of the Thames and the gothic steeples of Westminster. For the first few minutes Fenny felt a giddy sense of fear, but when Lion opened an alligator briefcase and began to check his accounts as calmly as if he sat at his desk in his office, she settled down to enjoy the flight. The deep tones of Zonar and Demetre drifted to her, but she knew they were speaking to each other in Greek, possibly keeping her name out of their conversation because Lion would hear them.

'Feeling more relaxed now we are in the air?' He gave her a brief look and the light through the windows caught in his eyes and made them even more startling in his dark face. 'I find this mode of transport much more convenient than travelling by plane. We can land on our own rooftop, did you know that?'

'No.' She attempted a slight smile. 'I know very little about your world, despite what you think of me.'

'I'm sure you aren't totally unaware of what has been written in the press about the secluded realm the Mavrakis family have created for themselves on the island of Petaloudes? It is fairly well known that we are a self-made clan, with a disinclination to let strangers into our stronghold.'

'And I am a stranger,' she said. 'I walked in without an invitation.'

'Let it not be forgotten, *kyria*, and don't come running to me if some members of my family refuse to accept you.'

'You refer to Demetre, don't you? I – I sense that he's shocked by me and doesn't intend to forgive me.'

'Can you blame him? He has been more sheltered from the hazards of life than Zonar, who is now a confirmed cynic about happiness; who snatches his pleasure with all the careless greed of a boy plucking fruit from another man's tree. You will not forget that he is now your brother!'

'Of course I shan't forget it, but I – I must have one friend at least.'

'Must you?' His eyes were gem-hard as they swept her face in the clear light through the observation windows. 'Come, you aren't going to pretend to me that you have need of any sympathy. You knew the risks you were taking when you took those vows that made you the wife of a Greek. We aren't a gentle people, so don't start feeling sorry for yourself.'

Suddenly he leaned close to her and his voice sank low in his throat. 'You surely weren't fool enough to hope for the emotional heights of a grand romance ... or did you harbour the even more foolish hope that ours would be a *mariage de convenance?*'

'Both would be forlorn hopes, wouldn't they?' she said. 'I didn't think beyond the moment, and then it was too late – like reaching out to a flame and thinking it wouldn't burn.'

'My dear, you aren't a child.' His mouth gave a little twist of scorn. 'Reaching for the flames, and trying to stroke lions, are the actions of infants and idiots. They aren't a believable excuse, so stop trying to convince me that you didn't know what you were doing. Applaud your own success. You made an angelic-looking bride, and last night you were – satisfactory.'

'Was I?' She dropped her glance to the bracelet on her wrist, and wondered what he would have whispered to Penela had she been sitting here beside him. 'I'm glad you didn't feel completely robbed.'

'A woman is a woman.' He shrugged his wide shoulders that to her touch last night had felt like hot silk and copper. 'The bargain we have made suits me well enough.'

He returned his attention to the batch of business papers he had brought with him, and Fenny stared blindly from the window beside her. That hateful bargain which she could hardly bear to think about, which he had every right to make and expect to be kept – if she had his child. It was a cruel way for him to have his revenge on her, and yet it was only to be expected of a man who had built his own stronghold and resented the invasion of his private world by a woman he had not selected to share it.

No matter how much love she gave him, he would never regard her as his true wife. She was the means to an end, and it was a source of sardonic satisfaction to him that he found a certain pleasure in her slim body. It was only her body that mattered to him; her feelings were as nothing.

A woman is a woman, he had said, shrugging his shoulders on love.

'Do you smoke, Fenella?' Zonar was leaning across to her with a gold cigarette case.

'No, she doesn't,' Lion said, without glancing up from his paperwork. 'Her breath and skin are proof of that.'

'Sweet, eh?' Zonar drawled, and his eyes looked directly into Fenny's a moment before he relaxed into his seat again. He lit a cigarette for himself, and Fenny knew that he was smiling a little to secret thoughts about her – a quiet girl who had been audacious enough to secure a rich husband for herself. He was intrigued by her, and his own loss of love had made him reckless in his dealings, for his young wife had died so tragically. In a way he could only forget by drowning his mind in affairs that brought him only a brief release from memory, adding all the time to his cynicism.

Now he contemplated the danger of making a pass at his brother's bride ... a girl his brother didn't love but undoubtedly owned.

Oh God! Fenny's heart felt weighted with problems. The last thing on earth she wanted was to be the cause of a rift between Lion and the young brother he had fought to make happy. She wanted a friendship but not a flirtation; needed one member of the Mavrakis family to make her welcome, but certainly not in the way Zonar contemplated.

Her fingernails plucked at her handbag, and she gave a little start when Lion gave her knuckles a tap with his fountain-pen. 'You'll break them,' he chided her. 'In that office where you worked did you ever do the accounts?'

'Occasionally,' she said, wondering what he was getting at.

'Are you any good at it?'

'I managed without getting the books in a muddle. I quite like figure work.'

'Excellent.' He handed her a folder with papers inside and took from the inside pocket of his jacket a gold pencil that matched his pen. 'See what you can do with these; they're figures relating to my restaurants in Athens but made out in English for the benefit of my accountant who happens to be British.'

Fenny took the folder and the pencil and realized that Lion was merely asking for her assistance in order to keep her mind occupied. She was curiously grateful to him and her smile was unconsciously sweet and warm. He stared at her a moment, then said curtly, 'Well, get on with it and earn a cup of coffee in a while.'

'Yes—' Her smile faltered and she bent over the folder, that little ache creeping back into her heart. Would he never, never look at her without that scornful twist at the edge of his mouth ... could she ever hope to have anything from him other than this hate and passion that he showed her?

Her fingers clenched his pen and she strove to concentrate on the columns of figures, determined to add them correctly and earn a little of his approval.

Time passed, the chugging of the helicopter and the

murmur of male voices drifting at the edge of Fenny's awareness. The mental work was proving the best medicine she could have asked for, and she was on the last page of figures when the aroma of coffee made her glance up to see that refreshments were being served.

'We're putting down at Nice for some fuel.' Lion handed her a cup of the delicious-smelling coffee. 'You'll see that we're over the blue seas if you glance from the window.'

The south of France! Fenny gazed down at the dazzling ocean and the glimpses of white beach and excitement clutched at her. England was well behind them, and she guessed that after this brief stopover they would be flying on straight to Greece.

As she drank her coffee, Lion checked her totals against his own. 'You are good,' he murmured. 'I shall know who to call on any time I have too much paperwork on my hands. Now you know, *kyria,* how much I can make from my rather swish *kafeneions.*'

At once, and she knew it was deliberate, he took the joy out of the hour and made the sun feel chilly. She refused to look at him, but she managed to say quite steadily, 'Yes, it must be satisfying to have such good business from your coffee shops.'

He gave a growl of a laugh and handed her a brown bread sandwich with a thick slice of ham jutting from the edges. 'So the little claws still have some scratch left in them, eh?'

'I should hope so – thank you.' The sandwich was as tasty as the coffee, and despite the heartache he made her feel, life with Lion seemed to put an edge on her appetite and she bit deeply into the bread and spicy ham. She saw him quirk a black brow and saw his eyes steal down over the skin of her neck in the opening of the pink shirt. His glance was like a touch, reminding her of last night, and promising again that maddening, sensuous delight that drowned her mind to everything but pure sensation.

Each time he took her in his arms he would be thinking ahead to that possible moment when she had to say to him: 'I'm going to have a baby!'

'Cake?' Zonar was leaning forward with slices from that magnificent cake which Fenny had last seen on the sideboard in her uncle's dining-room the night before the wedding. It was snow-white, covered in candy flowers, latticework, almonds and a pair of real silver bells. 'Come, Fenella, you must taste your own marriage cake.'

She knew that Zonar spoke lightly, without meaning to stab at her vulnerable feelings, but she felt her face go cold and white. 'It isn't my cake,' she said. 'We all know that, don't we!'

'All the same you will eat some,' Lion said firmly. 'It's customary.'

'Why?' she muttered. 'Is it a fertility rite? Will it help to ensure that I give my Greek husband a sweet-natured son?'

There was an instant, crushing silence as her words struck at each of the men. Heaven help her! She hadn't meant to reveal the depth of torment, but Lion drove her to it with his hardness of heart; not even last night had softened him a little towards her.

She tossed back her hair in the streaming light and it seemed fired about her face, and her eyes looking into Lion's wouldn't flinch as her nerves did.

'We can but hope that he will have a sweeter nature than his mother's. Open your mouth!' he gritted.

'I won't – I'm not a seal being thrown a fish!'

'You're obstinate, my dear.' His eyes were adamant, making her feel like a moth trapped in amber. 'Stop being childish and eat your cake – and like it.'

'Go to hell, Lion.' She said it deliberately, no longer caring a fig that his brothers were witness to every lack of tenderness between them. What did it matter? How was it possible to fool them into thinking that this marriage might hold some semblance of joy for a man tied to a woman he had been fooled into marrying? That for Lion was the unforgivable aspect, and he'd have her crawling on her knees before he was finished with her.

Well, he'd have to push her down, for she wouldn't drop to them and bow her head upon his boots, like some bond-slave of the old Byzantine courts.

She looked at his face and saw that Byzantine quality about him, wry, cruel and haunted.

'Would you like to go there?' His eyes were narrow and threatening slithers of hot gold in his dark face.

'I don't doubt that you could arrange it,' she said. 'There's something hubristic about you, isn't there, Lion? An arrogance of a godlike nature that forbids you to be weak and forgiving like other men.'

'Perhaps, brother, your wife would be happier to keep the slice of cake wrapped in its serviette.' It was Zonar who spoke, keeping his voice as impartial as possible. 'Women have these superstitions, eh? That you can't have your cake and eat it.'

'If she feels that it would choke her, then by all means let her have it in a serviette.' Lion turned his shoulder on her and poured more coffee for himself from the large flask. Fenny tried not to let her eyes be too grateful to Zonar, murmuring an almost inaudible word of thanks when he handed her the little package.

Demetre sat there in a stony silence, looking as if he'd like to slide open the door of the helicopter and push her out of their lives. She felt her limbs trembling, for there was violence in the Mavrakis brothers and she was at the centre of their various reactions to her. An unwanted wife

... an interloper ... a girl who stirred all the wrong emotions in Zonar.

She thrust the wrapped cake into her bag, and was utterly relieved when they put down at Nice and she was able to escape to a heliport ladies' lounge for a while.

There she sat in an armchair and felt the tension humming in her very veins. She opened her bag and counted her money ... there had been no time to take from the bank the cash she had saved for her holiday ... enough cash to have helped her get away from a situation that was becoming almost impossible to control. Her fingers clenched her thin wallet, and she felt an agonized sense of regret that she had ever meddled in Lion's life. What devil had stood at her elbow and urged her to put on that white lace dress left discarded by Penela across her bed? Was that dark demon dancing a jig on the remnants of the safe and tedious life she had left behind at Wimbledon?

She gave a start when the lounge attendant bent over her. The woman spoke in French and Fenny just about understood that she was asking if Madame was quite well.

'*Oui, merci.*' She conjured a smile of reassurance, and rising to her feet tidied her hair at the mirror, powdered her face, and braced her shoulders for the remainder of the journey to Petaloudes. She had made her bed and now she must lie on it with as good a grace as possible.

Slim, pink-clad, her courage re-charged, Fenny walked in the sun towards the gleaming cage of scarlet, where Lion stood a little apart from his brothers, smoking a cheroot in brooding silence. Fenny went straight to him and said quietly, 'I apologize for losing my temper. I'll try not to let it happen again, for I did promise to put on a show of wifely obedience.'

'We have merely proved that we can't live a lie.' He

shrugged his shoulders. 'Love is an emotion and it can't be put on like a cloak, or flung off for that matter. Well, Metre has already voiced what I feared would be thought; he accuses you of marrying me for mercenary reasons.'

'And you really believe it, don't you, Lion?'

'Yes.' He spoke curtly. 'What else is there for me to believe? You and I were veritable strangers to each other, who spoke no more than half a dozen words at your uncle's house. Would you pretend to care for a stranger?'

'No,' she admitted, and knew it would be hopeless to say that it hadn't mattered that she hardly knew him. There had been something about him that made him different from those boring, faceless wonders with their perpetual talk about cars, mortgages and easy women. Sometimes she had felt like yawning in their faces, and instead had worn her hair in a sexless bun and assumed the prim attitude of a girl who had no interest 'in that sort of thing'. It had worked like a charm, and she hadn't cared a jot that she was left alone to pay for her own cinema seats and the occasional meal at a restaurant.

The fact of men ... of love ... had not impinged until her cousin brought a tall, dark Greek into the house and shared with him the joke that her cousin Fenny was men-shy.

Yes, with Penela he had shared the small jokes, the quick-healed arguments, and the plans of a real engagement ... with Fenny he had shared only a meaningless marriage service, and a wedding night in which tenderness had played no part.

It was enough to make her weep with terror and pain, and instead she had to stand before him and assume an air of dignity, like one of those women of the revolution who held high the head until it rolled from under the steel knife.

His eyes were like pitiless steel, flicking across her bared neck.

'I think you'd like to mount my head on a spear,' she said, trying to speak lightly.

'Better where it is on your charming neck, I think.' Those taunting, wicked lights stole into his eyes. 'There are consolations even in a marriage such as ours, for me if not for you. But then, *melle mou*, you never earned a consolation prize from the cheating that you did.'

'No,' she said. 'I have no balm in Gilead, if that pleases you and adds to your own gratification.'

'It does, my dear. You will never know how it sweetens the lemon I must bite each time I look at you and hear again your sweet, cheating voice at my side in church, vowing to be a loving, devoted and obedient wife. It's a wonder the stone angels didn't stir into life and strike you with their swords.'

'They left that for you, Lion. You are the stone angel with steel in your every glance. It strikes me, you can be sure of that.'

'And burns you, *kyria*?'

'Just as if I were tied to a stake!'

'A witch, not a saint, my dear.'

'If you say so, *kyrie*.'

'I do, Fenella. I say it now, and every time we are alone. A white-skinned little witch who cast a spell over an entire congregation, her soul in flames.'

'Burning crisply like a *kebab*, I take it?'

'I hope it.' He gave his gravelly laugh and dropped his cheroot to the ground, his heel grinding it flat. 'It's as well that you keep a sense of humour, for I shan't be ever kind to you when it's so much more gratifying to be cruel. Hubristic you called me, and it's a better word than arrogant, for I don't bully without reason. I have reason enough with regard to you, sweetheart.'

'And will there never come a time when I can expect my punishment to be over?' she asked.

'It will end,' he touched her, pressing his fingers into her rib-cage, 'when you give me a son. You are very slim and it may hurt like hell.'

'You'll smile when I scream, won't you, Lion? You hate me that much?'

'You called me proud, didn't you?'

'Pride is your second name.'

'Then why the reproachful look? We reap what we sow.'

'And your harvest will be my – my baby, if I should have one?'

'Make it a son, *kyria*, and end your purgatory as soon as possible.'

'They made you from Greek stone, like a *kouros*.'

'A godlike youth?' He drew back his head and laughed aloud. 'Don't try flattery on me, my dear, I'm immune from it. Greek stone, yes, but not in the shape of a charming Adonis, not even when I was a youth. The Mavrakis looks went to the twins.'

'But the gods gave you other gifts, didn't they, Lion?'

'Yes, if you mean tenacity and a sharp brain.'

And other things, she thought, feeling those odd little nerves tightening like silk threads deep in her abdomen. Those imposing shoulders and that catlike walk, alert and yet infinitely assured. The golden fire of his eyes ... a compelling quality to his voice that seemed to vibrate in her bones, an inducement to fear and surrender at one and the same time.

He had a hard and striking charisma that made him far more dangerous than other men.

'You were born to enjoy conflict,' she said. 'It's the

Spartan in you and you know it. You hate me, yet you want my – child. Will you throw him from a clifftop if he should take after me?'

'It will be enough if he has your – beauty. The rest will come from me,' he said it with arrogant confidence. 'Love – hate, they are as close to each other as the skin upon the skeleton.'

'Really?' Her heart skipped several beats. 'Will you give my son the legendary advice of Sparta, "Come back with your shield, or on it"?'

'It has always been sound advice; men should be hard, and women good to look upon.'

'I'm happy, at least, that you don't find me hideous.' A smile drifted across her face. 'You Greeks worship the memory of Helen of Troy, yet you never let go of your male superiority. Women are born for your comfort, and it's to your male friends that you take your concerns.'

'Women can be so emotional, and Greek women at least like to be dominated and taken care of. Any Grecian girl will tell you that she lives to bear a son and to see him grow into a hard, proud man. Is it such a bad philosophy? In your own country, *kyria*, there would be less discontent in the hearts of the women if the men would remember their true role in life and cease to be so soft and easy-going. Were you so enamoured of these men?'

Fenny thought of the contempt they had aroused in her, and her response to this Greek male who represented a strength of will and body she had not encountered in all her twenty-two years.

Her eyes skimmed across the arresting width of shoulder ... she had fought with him and found him an opponent of hard, frightening determination, and she loved him for it.

Loved him, yet had to go on fighting with him, for that was what he wanted of her, his false and cheating bride.

87

'You believed that I had lovers,' she said.

'In that I was proved wrong, unless, of course, you were what is called a tease.' His eyes raked across her face. 'Were you?'

Had he asked that question of Penela, it would have been relevant and Fenny knew it. Even yet she could hear her cousin laughing, curled up on her bed as she related yet another easy conquest. 'Men are such fools,' she had been fond of saying, 'if you know how to string them along.'

'Would you believe me,' Fenny said quietly, 'if I denied being that sort of girl?'

'I look into your eyes, *kyria*, and I would be a fool to try and fathom their mystery – like smoke drifting over the morning seas – like the misty dusk creeping into the evening sky. A saint couldn't fathom your mystery!'

'Perhaps it takes a cynic?' Zonar had strolled up to them, and obviously he had overheard Lion's remark. 'A girl without mystery is like a gem without depth – like a dish without pepper. Right now Fenella reminds me of cool pink melon – mouth-watering.'

Lion gave him a sharp look, then took Fenny abruptly by the elbow.

'It's time for us to go,' he said. 'I feel as if I have been away from Petaloudes too long.'

'Your island of butterflies,' Fenny murmured.

'The only real and valued beauty in my life.' His voice was harsh, his hand painful as he assisted Fenny into the helicopter. 'Remember it!'

'I'll remember everything,' she said, her voice fading to a whisper.

A few minutes later the scarlet cage lifted into the air, the blades whirling into the sunlight like huge cutting knives.

CHAPTER FOUR

A silence lay over the sea, a hushed and solemn moment of intense beauty. Everything was cool and dusky, with great streaks of colour streaming across the sky from the falling sun.

Falling towards the sea, making way for the stars.

The Alouette hovered above the island, the blades whirling as the scarlet and silver helicopter came down gradually upon the natural plateau that lay between the terraces of fruit and the *kastello* itself.

The rooftop of the island, dominated by the white house overlooking the blue Aegean and the wild beauty of the coastline.

'We are home!' Lion said it in a voice that was strange to Fenny, for it was alive with a passionate joy. 'Home!'

She looked at him and saw his mouth silently scorn her for thinking for one moment that he included *her* in his heartfelt gladness to be here. She braved his look, proudly and quietly. She mustn't show him, this man her husband, the depth of his power to tear her feelings as the blades of the Alouette tore the air before settling down with a wrenching roar of its engine, until it gradually fell into a silence that came as a great relief.

Now the stars were spreading their witch-fire across the velvety sky, and Fenny realized how many miles she was from *Mon Repos*, her uncle's house, with its sedate neatness and carefully mown lawn, the flower borders as orderly as if tended by a barber.

Petaloudes ... wild, wild Greek island, an inhabited slab of rock in a great bowl of glowing wine. High cliffs and fragrant herbs, giving off their incense after the heat of the day. Broken statuary of silvery stone and death-pale marble. The pulse-beat of the cicadas drumming away in the gathering darkness.

Here were the scents and shadows of old pagan Greece, eternal among its ruins, and the high-built house of the island's present 'pasha'.

'Man must live on earth as though he had only one more day to enjoy its light.' The philosophy of Apollo, which seemed to fit Lion as closely as his sun-dark skin and the polo shirt gleaming white in the dusk as he swung from the cabin of the helicopter and stood a moment breathing deeply his native air.

Original and fierce, thought Fenny, feeling her every nerve respond to every hard line of him, from his flung back head to the way he stood on Greek soil, supple and balanced. Always his own master, until she had dared to step into his path and shake a little his belief in his own omnipotence.

His house like a white sun-temple was set among giant olive trees, towering cypresses and groves of citrus. The walls were like rough icing, and arched windows were set deep in the stone. It had the same hard grandeur of its master, and coloured light glowed through its windows like flame in a forge.

It had lofty rooms, seclusion, and wondrous views of sea, sky, and the twinkling lights of the islanders' hillside houses.

'Welcome to *Galazia Kastro*.' It was Zonar who welcomed Fenny to the Blue Castle – and the name puzzled her until she realized that this Mavrakis stronghold hung like an eagle's nest high above the sea, so that from every angle the blue water would be seen, rippling and murmuring in the sunlight and the moonlight.

Frosted gin and tonics were waiting for the brothers,

held upon a tray in misted glasses by a manservant in a spotless white jacket. For Fenny there was a cool, orange-coloured drink that tasted of mixed fruits and a dash of wine. It was perfectly delicious, and excitement fluttered deep in the pit of her stomach as she stood there in the cool hall and heard the brothers roar in unison: *'Stin iyia sou! Patrida! Yasou – yasou!'*

A great dark staircase arched across the hall, an immense mosaic of tiles worn to a silky smoothness and formed into an ancient pattern from the heart of the orient. Fenny was led up the stairs by a woman in a long dark dress, away from the men, to the sanctuary of an apartment where the silence was like a benediction after the combined excitements of the day.

The woman gazed at her, the bride of the *kyrios*, with curious dark eyes set in a face deeply etched by sun-lines. She was unable to speak English, but she murmured some words that sounded friendly enough to Fenny, and so she smiled and attempted one or two of the Greek words she had learned for her Cretan holiday which had turned into a strange, bitter-sweet honeymoon.

Her attempt at the language and her accent seemed to amuse the woman, for she smilingly shook her head, and then surprised Fenny by reaching for her hand and turning it palm upwards. For several moments she studied the palm, which looked very pale against the tanned fingers of the housekeeper. Then she glanced up into Fenny's eyes and held up a single finger, but what she said was a mystery.

'Den katalaveno,' Fenny managed in passable Greek, letting the woman know that she didn't understand what it was she had seen in her hand.

'Rodakino.' The woman suddenly touched her cheek, leaving a quick, rough sensation of well-worked fingers against Fenny's face. A peach! Soft like a peach? And

again that gesture with the forefinger, somehow earthy in its implication, and suddenly hitting Fenny with its meaning. She was a bride, and to Greeks a newly wed woman had a most important function in their eyes ... to produce for her husband as soon as possible the child that proved his manhood.

One child! The gipsy-like woman saw in her palm a single birth ... oh, but it had to be mere foolish superstition, for how could anyone have the power to see into the future!

Fenny smiled and shook her head.

'*Malista.*' There was insistence in the Greek eyes, and then she turned away and indicated the suitcases and the deep cupboards, implying that she would unpack for the *kyria*. Fenny produced the keys from her handbag and unlocked the cases, and once again she attempted a few words in Greek, asking the woman her name.

'Kassandra,' she was told, and Fenny all but gave a laugh at the sheer absurdity of it all ... was she really to believe that this woman was a modern-day prophetess, who had the power to tell her that she would have but one child?

Islands were strange, unearthly places, and the people who lived on them had unworldly ways and beliefs in all kinds of magic, but she came from England and she had to cling to her own kind of logic ... she dared not believe that Kassandra might have the gift of second-sight, for she might see other, even more disturbing things ... the absence of love in this new life of Fenny's, and in the end her departure from this white house high above the sea of Aphrodite.

Fenny made the Greek woman understand that she now wished to be left alone, and after the door of the suite had closed behind her dark-clad figure (she was presumably a widow, for it was well known that Greek women took to wearing black after the death of a husband, to signify that the sun of life had faded for them) the new, young, unloved mistress of the Blue Castle took herself on a tour of exploration of this large and very beautiful suite high in one of the square towers of the house – long ago the abode of a Turk who had probably had a number of girls kept here for his sole amusement.

She looked around her and saw screens of woodwork so finely carved they looked as if made of dark silky lace. The bed was like a huge divan built upon a dais, with sheer netting hooked back at the head of it, and with rugs at either side woven of many colours. The bed-quilt was of embroidered silk that made a whispering sound as she ran the tips of her fingers across it ... whispers of harem days that crept closer as she thought of Lion's regard for her.

This was his *donjon* – his lord's tower, in which she would live with him the most intimate part of their strange marriage.

She thought of that imperious corsair smile that sometimes touched his mouth, and she knew that deep in his blood there was a strain of the Turk, and it would amuse that part of him to keep her in an apartment which in its mesh-work and its jewelled lamps, and its subtle aroma of the orient, suggested the kept woman rather than the wife.

The rooms were connected by wide arches inset with beautiful wrought-iron doors, and the one adjoining the bedroom had a hand-painted ceiling and a fine mesh of carved woodwork screening the windows, beside which stood a great fan-back chair with a cushioned seat.

It was a fascinating room, with a jewel-slotted *lampada* glowing in a wall alcove before an icon in a silver frame. In another alcove stood an urn painted black and white with demon-like figures and dancing goats.

Pagan worship and a belief in the dark forces of life. Crystal windchimes made a soft and lovely sound as Fenny touched them, and with a sigh between guilt and gladness that she was here at all, she sat down in the fan-back chair and the height of the fan made her feel small as she leaned her head against the woven cane.

Her hand reached to a little inlaid table and she took a grape from the bunch that lay there on a dish, dusty velvet against the silver. As she ate the grape she noticed the chased ciborium, a drinking cup like a water-lily, and the lidded jug with a long Turkish spout. She leaned forward and lifted the jug, pouring into the cup some more of that cool sparkling fruit drink which had welcomed her to the house – in the traditional Greek manner.

A hard people, and yet with a graciousness so out of place, so lost to life in her own country. She drank from the silver ciborium, and told herself that if she could react and behave like Lion's harem girl, then she might find a measure of contentment. The guilt clamped down on her heart when she thought of herself as his wife . . . she could never be his true wife, for mere words in a church didn't make it so.

What did they put into this drink, for it had a relaxing effect on her, so she could wait here like this for Lion and not be a nervous, pacing creature in that room of the great, silky divan which she must share with him.

Here she absorbed the silence and the scents of the night stealing in through the mesh-work that replaced glass in the windows. This warm, vital, powerfully scented land, where in the olive yards the black, writhing branches of the trees were hung with glossy fruit. Where in the groves the drops of bitter-gold that were the lemons grew by the thousand and cast their pungent odour into the night.

The Blue Castle could have been heaven on earth for

her, but instead it had to be a paradise from which she would be cast for plucking the forbidden fruit.

She had deceived, she had lied, and she could never confess to Lion that she had done so out of love for him. He scorned her love ... her body appealed to the male genes that were rampant in him, but his sense of forgiveness had been forged in Sparta, where long ago for lesser crimes than hers women had been stoned in the public square.

Even in England she had sensed in Lion the savagery of primitive emotions not all that deep beneath his tawny skin ... that moment in the helicopter still lingered, when he had demanded that she choke on the cake he had wished to share with Penela. Those tiny bells of real silver had been meant to denote joy, but now they stood for slave bells! He meant it to be that way, that she be a slave to his demands, whether she liked it or not.

She had no choice ... love gave her none at all. Now they had arrived at the Blue Castle she knew how much she wanted to remain here. The place caught at the strings of her heart and gripped them. In every way she felt transported back into the past ... a female carried off from her home to give pleasure to a pasha, while it should please him to be by turns caressing and cruel.

In a bitter moment she might weep alone and cry into her cushions that she was his chattel, but she wouldn't have exchanged any of the bitter-sweetness for those dull days and empty nights of her life in England.

That expectant shiver ran all through her, and her instincts must have been attuned to Lion even before she saw him standing tall at the wrought-iron door into the softly lit room where she sat half lost in the fan-back chair.

As he stepped into the room the smoke of a Turkish cigarette wafted to her, creating an aromatic haze through which his eyes had a leonine glow, intensified by the blackness of his lashes and his brows. 'This is part of the old *haremlik*,' he said. 'I wired that the rooms be prepared for you – do you like them?'

'I find them fascinating,' she admitted. 'What is behind that silk hanging?'

She gestured at the far wall, where the silk hung in a primitive splash of colour and design.

He moved across to it, walking in that lithe, silent way of a creature in a jungle rather than a house. He drew aside the hanging and disclosed a carved panel. He pressed the eye of a prancing wild horse carved into the cedarwood and the panel slid open and there beyond it were the lights and furnishings of a large sitting-room.

'This is the secret door from the pasha's apartment,' he said, a droll note in his voice. 'He would come to his favourite when he felt like it, and the secrecy would, I suppose, add a little spice to the adventure. Men in those days were unlikely to regard women as anything more than a form of amusement, and the girl would have been kept like a bird in a cage. If she dared to enter the pasha's rooms through the panel she would be severely punished, and the outer doors of the *haremlik* itself were always kept locked by a great key held in the possession of the eunuch who guarded them.'

'Was she never allowed an airing?' Fenny asked.

'In the company of the eunuch, no doubt, and also out on the private *moussandre*. Come, let me show you!'

Fenny rose from her chair and followed him through the wooden meshwork that opened out from the windows like doors. Starlight flooded down and she found herself upon a balcony that hung above the lemon groves and the sloping cliffs to the sea. Its furniture was cane-woven and its railings were entangled in a bell-vine giving off a heavenly scent that mingled with the ocean tang, the lemons and the pine trees.

'*Moussandra*,' he said again. 'A little room, exclusive to the occupant of the *haremlik*, whether she remained a night ... or a year.'

Fenny's hands caught at the iron railings and her fingers crushed the flower bells. Her heart raced in her breast as Lion came to stand right behind her, so tall, so firmly muscled, so impossible for her to reach with the love that clamoured in her veins.

In the glow of the stars she could just make out the dark spears of the cypress trees. Countless fireflies shimmered in the air, flying points of pure green, and Fenny stood taut by the parapet iron, Lion's powerful, silent figure behind her. She heard the croaking of night creatures among the tall trees, and then a flicker of red flame joined the green as Lion tossed his cigarette far down over the railings. His arms came around her and she was turned to him as easily as a leaf on a branch.

'You should feel at home in this apartment, *kyria*. In every way it seems to suit you, don't you agree?'

'As the wife of a Greek must I always agree with my husband?' she asked.

'Why, does the atmosphere of this place seem to bring out the Eastern autocracy in me, and the sense of submission in you? Wife – husband! They're such meaningful words, aren't they? Designed to mean so much, yet in our case they mean so little.'

'The pasha with his slave,' she said, forcing that light note into her voice. 'But for all that I don't intend to crawl on my knees to you, *kyria*. You'd have to strike me down to that level, low as you already think I am.'

'I have every right in the world to think you – well, let us admit it, you stooped to conquer, did you not?'

'I very much doubt that anyone could conquer you, Lion, least of all a woman.'

'True.' He gave his gravelly laugh and encircled her pale throat with his hand, holding the slimness to him as he might the stem of a goblet from which he meant to drink to the very dregs. He held her face to the starlight and studied her eyes and her features framed in the golden hair that spilled over his skin. 'Zonar noticed that you were beautiful, and I didn't even notice you. That must signify something, eh?'

'You were too occupied with—' Fenny swallowed, for it suddenly seemed terribly hard to say Penela's name, 'with my cousin. Why should you notice the mouse of the family?'

'Why indeed?' His fingers ran across the smooth skin of her neck and paused where her pulse was beating in time with her quick beating heart. 'How madly runs your pulse — are you so afraid of my touch?'

'Well, more than once you have threatened to break my neck, and you don't make idle threats, do you?'

'Not as a rule, but being a Greek who learns early to know the value of assets, I don't go in for discarding something that still has profit in it, for me. On one level, my dear, I find you rather distracting, and on another I have regard for that certain bargain we made, and if I broke your lovely neck I'd be killing the goose who might lay for me a golden egg.'

'How delightfully you put it,' she said, and his stroking fingers were making her feel weak at the knees, so that she wanted to clutch at him and then give way to the weakness in the security of his arms. But that was a luxury only to be enjoyed by a woman who was loved; all she could do was suffer his mocking caresses and the glint of possessiveness in his eyes as he looked her over.

'Shall we be joining your family for dinner?' she asked, and it was impossible not to shiver as he ran his fingers down her spine, leaving a trail of sensation that made her bite her lip.

'We are a newly married couple, *melle mou*, and to Greek people that means only one thing, that we desire to be alone with each other. No, we shan't be joining the family tonight. Food is being brought to us – that is when I ring the service bell to give the signal that we wish to eat. Right now my appetite is for you, my wife, and I don't have to ring for you, I just have to snap my fingers!'

He gave a soft, cynical laugh and his arms were suddenly as hard as iron around her, crushing her to him, careless of hurting her. The stars looked down, drowning in her eyes as her head was thrust back against his arm in an aching, bitter-sweet surrender to his hard lips.

With that easy, almost terrifying strength he carried her from the *moussandra* and straight through into the room where that divan lay in its shadows.

All that Fenny was aware of was Lion's hands, his mouth, his dark presence beside her on the bed. Her pulses had set up a thunder, and she let the sensuous waves lift her and take her ... Aphrodite of the foam.

The robe clung in silken folds about her young body, her white skin softly shadowed within the golden charm of the caftan. Her legs were curled beneath her in the depths of the scarlet chair, and she ate the roasted quail as Lion did, holding it in her fingers and tearing the meat from the small bones. The fragrance of coffee mingled with the tang of the food, cooked in herbs, and Fenny ate with a hunger that shouldn't have amazed her, for she had not eaten much since breakfast.

'Strange,' murmured Lion, wiping his fingers on a napkin that was a startling white against his dark skin, 'a man and a woman make love, and afterwards the woman is a small girl again, eager as a child at a picnic, innocent-looking as if on a convent outing with a good Sister in charge. More than strange – truly amazing. Who would believe to look at you, *kyria*, that you have so much passionate resistance in you – and so much fire in the fine, white English body. I thought the *Anglika* was a cool creature, with water in her veins.'

'Surely not Penela?' Fenny murmured, slicing into a tomato that was deliciously stuffed with meat and rice.

'I never knew Penela as I know you,' he rejoined, and her heart seemed to turn in her breast at his obvious meaning. She gave him a quick look, and colour stormed into her cheeks when she found his eyes waiting for that look, sardonic and yet with those tiny leaping fires still alive in the dark centres of the gold-ringed pupils.

'Did you think that I had leapt the fence before the gate was opened?' he drawled. 'The Greek likes a virgin beside him at the altar. He likes to think that his bride is pure as sun-dried linen, fresh-fallen snow, soft white rice.' Infinite mockery lurked in his deep voice.

'And it doesn't matter that the bridegroom is well versed in the art of – seduction?' She tried to be as scornful as he.

'What girl would want a fumbling fool on her wedding night? It is a traumatic enough experience for a bride without any knowledge or finesse on the part of the man to make it bearable.' His teeth gleamed as he bit into a stuffed tomato, and he chewed enjoyably with his eyes still intent upon Fenny. 'Admit, *melle mou*, that I didn't make a total wreck of you, either last night or tonight?'

The colour burned deeper in her cheeks and she had to fight not to drop her gaze like a shy fool. She shook her head. 'No one could accuse you of being a brute,' she said. 'But you are a believer in male superiority, aren't you?'

'Am I?' He shrugged his fine shoulders in the heavy silk of his robe. 'A man is physically stronger than a woman, and sometimes he has a shrewd and more logical mind, but we Greeks respect the fact that a woman can create within her delicate body a living replica of the man who has possessed her. Does that make me a male chauvinist son of a sow, as I believe the American female terms it?'

Fenny had to smile, for to look at this man had a lithe arrogance that seemed to imply that women were but playthings to him. But it wasn't really true of him or his fellow Greeks. It was a creed of the Western world that life was a game and women merely players! Back in England she had rarely come upon a man who thought it rather a miracle that from an embrace of passion a child had its birth. Men back home seemed more concerned that girls should be on the Pill and available for everything except the act of creation.

'There are surprising aspects to you, Lion,' she said. 'I suppose we are learning a few things about each other.'

'That will be inevitable, my dear.' He sliced a piece of honey cake and held it out to her. 'Will you eat this from my hand without looking as if it will poison you?'

'Thank you.' She took the cake and vivid again was the recollection of his anger over the wedding cake. She bit into the honey cake and found it mouth-watering. 'You have an excellent cook, *kyrie*. You like good things, don't you?'

'I like them, and thanks to providence and the sweat of my labours I can now afford them. A man should earn the good things of life, not be handed them on a plate. Of course, it must be remembered that the best honey in the world is from the wild bees in the maquis-scented hills of Greece. There in the springtime the earth is covered with anemones, tiny orchids, asphodels and flowering grasses, and each step that a man takes crushes herbs into a wild fragrance. True there are barren parts to the country, but even where the temples and pediments have fallen, and where the lion heads crumble into dust, there is a certain beauty.'

'You love your land, don't you, *kyrie*?'

'*Patrida*, love of the fatherland.' He leaned back with his coffee and his robe fell open against the warm dark skin of his shoulders. 'I would have no other land despite its frictions and its unrest. I would live and die nowhere but here.'

'Tell me some of your Greek customs,' she urged, for she felt that if she learned something of his country she would learn a little more about him. It wasn't enough to have lain in his arms; she wanted to try and reach the heart and soul that lay within the hard body that had been so close to her; closer than anyone ever had been and yet with a barrier holding her aloof from the innermost part of him.

He gave her a quizzical look and his fingers played with the crystal stopper of the cognac decanter before he withdrew it and poured the deep gold spirit into the cut-glass bowls. It made them shimmer like jewels, catching the lamplight as he transferred one of them to her hand.

'So you are curious about my kind of people,' he said, and he raised his brandy snifter to his well-cut nostrils and slowly rolled the liquid around the glass. '*Stin iyia sou!*'

She echoed him, but without his clipped intonation that made the Greek words so meaningful, and she saw his lips quirk as he took the brandy into his mouth and leaned back his head as if to enjoy the warm sensation down his hard brown throat. Each of his actions seemed to her like the vital, sensuous movements of a sleek lion, and she felt that she was slowly burning in the look he gave her across the rim of his glass.

'Many of our customs are part of the old days and they

survive mainly because we wish it so, because we are a people like our land, harsh and yet enduring; hard like marble and yet with a core of flame. The firstborn son of a Greek household knows that his lot will always be a little harder than that of his brothers and sisters, for he must help provide for them. Our girls are almost born with the idea that they must have a man and a home, and their greatest joy is to bear a son. We have no respect for titles and snobbery, only for success; our feelings are deep, and I think more sincere than the more sophisticated Western races. We don't weep easily, for we are never quite out of touch with the fundamental sadness in the human soul. You will often see Greeks with the worry-beads in their sun-weathered hands; it is an old Byzantine habit, for if you count your worries you may also find that some of the beads are for a blessing.'

His fingers played over the facets of his brandy bowl and his eyes smiled in a deep, subtle way as he regarded Fenny's intentness in the scarlet chair, the way she listened to him with an absorbed silence that was almost childlike. Her hair and her fairness of skin were intensified against the fabric of the charmingly patterned caftan reaching to her ankles.

'You astonish me,' he said. 'Do you know the legend of Aphrodite – that she had the power to renew her chastity in the sea? I look at you and I see an illusion of that innocence – honey on your lips and pale fingers that surely didn't stab their nails into my shoulders.'

'All the wishing in the world won't make me quite the harlot that you believe me to be,' she said. 'Is everything for Greeks so harshly black and white, with no half-tones? Are your judgments made on tablets of stone?'

'There have been witches as well as martyrs who have stood in the flames and declared their innocence right up to the moment of supreme agony. You could be one or the other, and I shall enjoy the game of finding out.'

He leaned forward and his dusky-gold eyes were shadowed by his lashes, sensuously amused by this game that he played with her. 'My Cyrene, are you not, the girl who fought with a lion? Did you think, little fraud, that it would be an easy thing to do, to live with a Greek and make a fond fool of him with your gold hair and your slim white body? It isn't quite that easy, is it?'

'I never thought for one moment that you'd be an easy man to live with,' she said, and she could feel her toes curling inward as his eyes ran downwards into the neck of her robe ... the deliberately insolent look of a man who would take her whenever it suited him, as he might a fig or a lemon from the trees in his groves. He didn't have to whisper words of love, or care if her eyes showed fear of him. Her feelings were as the pith and stem of the fruit – unregarded.

'One thing I'll say for you, my girl, you don't cringe from me, you face me squarely.' His teeth glimmered in a half-smile. 'Is it the courage of hope or desperation, now that you find your rich Greek none too pliable?'

'Pliable?' She broke into a spontaneous laugh. 'It would take a fool to think you were easily influenced. You are supple in body, *kyrie*, but inflexible in mind. Like a Turkish scimitar, I think, that cuts so swiftly that it's only seconds afterwards that the agony is felt.'

'Agony?' He arched his brow as he reached into a cedarwood box for a slim cigar whose leaf crackled in his fingers as he pierced the end and spun the lighter into flame. 'You don't mind the smoke of a cigar?'

'Would it matter if I did?' She still held her brandy bowl in her hands, rather like a supplicant holding a chalice, a shining wing of hair falling down against her neck. Her eyes looked dark blue in the lamplight, big pools in her face that collected the mockery from his glance.

'You aren't that prudish,' he said, and smoke drifted from his ironical lips as he relaxed into the comfortable hold of his chair. 'I might once have thought so, but I have since discovered that your air of demure self-effacement was but a mask behind which the real Fenella was waiting to emerge. I think I am beginning to know the real person behind the drawn-back hair and the downcast eyes. How well you played the role of the spinsterish cousin, appearing to be so disinterested in men.'

'It was true!' A little of that agony he could evoke was there like a dark shadow in Fenny's eyes ... no one could hurt her as Lion could, for no one had ever meant this much to her. Men! They had been shadows on the edge of her life, meaningless and unwanted. And then at last when she did wake up to love, it was tormenting rather than rapturous.

'Certainly true that you were a spinster,' he drawled. 'Didn't men find you as attractive as they found Penela?'

'I never cared one way or the other.' Her fingertips pressed so hard against the facets of the brandy bowl that they felt bruised ... bruised as her feelings in Lion's grip. 'I never regarded men as being anything to run after ... I left that sort of thing to – to Penela.'

'Meaning that she likes to flirt?' Smoke wreathed about his face and gave him a slightly sinister look. 'Do you imagine I didn't know that a number of men had found her desirable? It would have been hard to fathom if she had not attracted their attention. Such wondrously bright hair and a nature that sparkles. Men would be inclined to overlook you, my dear, in her company.'

'And you honestly believed that I minded?' When Fenny thought of her life at *Mon Repos* she could have laughed, or wept, that anyone could imagine that she had lived in an agony of envy of her more outgoing cousin.

She had been tolerated in her uncle's home, and in her turn she had endured Penela's everlasting tales of battles lost and won in the back seats of all the most up-to-date cars. She had sometimes thought of renting a small flat, but rentals were so high and the available accommodation so unattractive. Her roof at Uncle Dominic's was small, but it overlooked the rose garden, and she was left alone much of the time to enjoy her own company.

Her own company had been sufficient ... she hadn't known until Lion Mavrakis walked into *Mon Repos* that her feelings could be so disturbed; that her dreams could be haunted by a man who barely looked at her when he had the scintillating Penela for his very own ... or so it had seemed at that time.

'I think you must have minded,' he said curtly. 'You lost precious little time in grabbing what she chose to discard – that will always be the venom in our cup of wine, my dear. Our time together will always be more bitter than sweet.'

Fenny had no answer to give him, for there was too much shattering truth in what he said. She raised her brandy bowl to her lips, needing to find a little courage even if the kind found in cognac was rather like the blind faith of those who tried to walk on water.

The soft ticking of the bedside clock was sister to the silence, and the aroma of his cigar mingled with the fragrance of the brandy. Fenny felt the two of them stealing to her brain and easing just a little the ache of her unhappiness. Lion's opinion of her was cast in bronze and couldn't be smashed ... it could only be melted down ... melted to pure blazing emotion that would scorch his resentment into ash.

There wasn't a hope in hell of that happening ... a single glance was enough to reveal how adamant was the Lion that she loved.

His lean face was a mask of detachment through the haze of his cigar smoke, and Fenny felt certain that he was thinking of Penela and her carefree gaiety. All his life he had worked so hard, and Fenny could understand why he had wanted to grab at a sunbeam ... she could almost feel the deep hard disappointment in him that the brightness had slipped from his grasp, and that she had made it impossible for him to pursue Penela to New York.

He was foremost a Greek and even a powerful desire for a woman was incomparable when it came to his obligations to his Grecian sense of honour, self-respect, and allegiance to the laws of his church.

A marriage was binding. His mind and heart might be reaching out for Penela, but it was Fenny whom he must treat as a wife in front of other people.

In private it was a different matter. In private he could be as cruel as he liked, and she had no defence against him.

Her nerves jarred when he suddenly shot a look at her, and with a downward stabbing motion put out his cigar in an ashtray. 'Do you have to wear that suffering-angel look on your face?' he demanded. 'It's one hell of a pity that I go with the house and its trappings, but you'll have to smile and bear it.'

'Is there any need to be profane?' she asked, hating him and loving him for his harsh way of speaking to her. Penela was no angel, she wanted to cry at him. Penela was well used!

'Profanity, my dear, just about makes it possible for me to have you here without breaking your lily-white neck.'

'It's a threat you're fond of, Lion. Why not carry it out?'

'I'm tempted, believe me.' His lips were thin with his smouldering rage, and then suddenly they were smiling just a little, taking that sensuous curve. 'Hate you I might, but that's when my mind is in control of me. When I think of what you've done to my life, it would be an inordinate pleasure to snap your neck in my hands. But as I said once before, a wrung goose is no use to me, and there are other pleasures to be had from you.'

He stood up and came towards her. He jerked her to her feet and she felt her head spin, making her stumble against him. 'Has the cognac gone to your legs?' He laughed softly and loosened the girdle of her robe, moving the soft silk aside so he could bury his face in her soft, warm skin. Fenny heard him catch his breath as he slid his lips into the silky hollow of her shoulder.

'You're a cheating, white-skinned devil, but by the Virgin I want you! The feel of you, the shape of you – a woman to help celebrate the fact that tonight I am back on my island. Only here are the stars like fire and the air like wine – it is here that a son of Greece should be quickened into life. You take my meaning, *melle mou?*'

She took it straight to her heart – dear heaven, she dare not have his son, the child who would end it all for her, the bitter and the sweet of being here on Lion's island.

She began to struggle in his arms. 'No!' The word tore from her throat. 'Lion, please leave me alone! I beg of you—'

'You may beg, my dear, but I have no intention of listening to you.' He swung her savagely up into his arms and mounted the steps to the divan, and with a desperation born of her love Fenny fought him like a mad thing, pounding him with hands that felt puny against his strong, inflexible shoulders.

'Resistance only adds to the sport,' he taunted her. 'I never did like the cold, passive type, and it matters not all to me that this excess of emotion is not that of a woman passionately in love. Your struggles only add to the attractive disorder of your person, and inevitably you will tire before I do.'

'Y-you have no heart,' she gasped, her fingers clenched in his black hair as he pressed his lips to sentient nerves alive and leaping under her skin. How much longer could she resist this overwhelming desire to give in to everything that she felt for him; this longing to stroke his firm skin and press her lips to his body. It was sheer hell pretending she didn't want him when every particle of her was longing for his touch.

'How can you say I have no heart when you can surely feel it beating?' His lips moved in a smile against her throat. 'This is our real honeymoon night, and I shall make you remember every moment of it. Now you will kiss me and stop tossing about like a stranded fish.'

'Y-you'll have to make me.' She was so at the mercy of her emotions that she was shaking in his arms, and the tears of her secret misery were suddenly spilling down her cheeks. She had sworn that she would never give him the satisfaction of her tears, but they wouldn't be held back. They came from that aching place in her heart, empty of the assurance of a woman wanted for herself.

She had asked for this, and now that she had it – a sob broke from her and she just couldn't stop the tears from spilling on to his skin.

'You are being a child, you know.' He clasped her face in his hands and made her look at him through the blinding, stinging tears. 'Is my touch so utterly hateful to you – come, tell me!'

And it was then that she had a terrible choice – she could have said truthfully that his touch could never be hateful even if he chose to beat her with his hands. But if she feigned dislike, fear, repugnance, he might leave her alone and not insist on the one thing that would set them apart ... not for a night but for always.

109

'I – I'm so tired,' she whispered. 'I just want to sleep—'

'Do you?' He stroked the tumbled hair away from her hot wet face, and in the lamplight she looked young and dispirited. 'I am perhaps being thoughtless and rather too harsh, but you knew what you were taking on and you have no one to blame but yourself.'

'I know—' She wiped the back of her hand across her face. 'You don't have to keep reminding me. I've done a bad thing a-and I've got to pay for it.'

'One way or the other.' He stared down at her, at the wet marks glistening on her face and streaking her temples. Her hair lay in tousled wings against the silk pillows, and the wet darkness of her lashes fluttered against her flushed cheeks, and about her young mouth lay tiny shadows of pain. The lamp burned softly at the bedside and its shaded gold light mingled with her hair.

'This time you are not acting, are you?' he said. 'The tears and the fear are genuine, and I have never gone in for rape.' Lean and lithe, he arose from the divan and stood tall beside it, tightening the cord of his robe. 'Sleep alone – tonight. *Kalinikta.*'

She couldn't return his goodnight, for her throat hurt too much, and she listened in tired defeat (for this was no victory) as he turned out the lamp and left the room, vanishing like a dark shadow through the secret door into his own rooms. As the panel slid into place, Fenny turned into her pillows with a moan of sheer aching distress of mind and body.

What could be more distressing than to be in love and to be no more than a piece of merchandise to the one man in the entire world?

She had wanted with her every nerve and fibre the passionate aliveness of being in Lion's arms, part of him even if he locked her out of his heart. But she also shrank from the very thought of what such passion could produce.

Already she could be having a child ... last night and earlier tonight she had belonged to him and known the ultimate thrill of being lost to the world and wholly surrendered to him.

Now he believed that she hated the vital passions of his warm and powerful body. So warm and strong ... so sure and exciting.

Fenny groaned and drove her fingernails into the silk coverlet as she had driven them into his shoulders. 'Lion ...' She breathed his name and remembered his strong, work-hardened hands on her skin, playing over her as if she were porcelain, and then suddenly almost savage but never to the actual point of bruising.

Restless rather than weary, she slipped off the bed and pushed her feet into slippers embroidered with tiny silk bats and butterflies, and tightening the girdle which Lion had loosened she wandered out on to the *moussandra* and walked to the railed parapet. She seemed to walk through shards of silver, for the stars overhead were as bright as if afire. Stars like jewels that no one could steal, or lock away, or wear against white skin.

She could smell the citrus groves that lay in terraces above the sea, and she breathed the bitter-almond fragrance that came from oleander flowers probably massed in the garden below this little railed room of a pasha's favourite.

And then as she stood there, still as a piece of marble statuary in the starlight, there came stealing to her the sound of a Greek mandolin playing a lullaby from the very heart of Greece itself, wooed out of the instrument from heavenly strings.

She listened enthralled, her fingers crushing the flowers

that draped the parapet. Who was it who played the music ... was it played to the motherless little son of Zonar?

For minutes on end the music filled the silence with its magic, and then it faded away and Fenny felt strangely alone again. Cut off from real intimacy with this Greek family, never to feel that she was part of its joys and its sorrows.

Her heart beat fast with apprehension of the future, and now in the silence she caught the sound of the sea splashing over the rocks and slapping itself against the walls of the cliffs. It seemed as if all her life she had been waiting to come to a place like Petaloudes, but there had been nothing to warn her that she would pay a high price for making her dream come true.

'It isn't quite so easy as you thought,' Lion had mocked her. 'Making a fond fool of a Greek husband.'

Had she dared to hope that she might teach him to love her? Perhaps she had, but now that hope felt like a dead weight in her breast. All of this might be her dream, but Lion's was far away in New York ... it was on Penela that he had set his heart.

In a while Fenny returned to the bedroom and crawled in lonely coldness beneath the covers. The room lay in darkness but for the glimmer of the *lampada* in the icon alcove, a pagan form of worship with its own curious beauty. Fenny might have prayed to the Virgin to grant her a little happiness, but she didn't really believe that she had earned it. She had stood in Penela's shoes, but they didn't fit her. Somehow the myth had gone all wrong and the glass slipper didn't belong to Cinderella.

Fenny curled down against the pillow which still bore the imprint of Lion's dark head and she fell asleep in the arms of an illusion.

CHAPTER FIVE

In the weeks that followed her arrival on the island Fenny grew accustomed to the routine of the *kastello*, a word which meant sea castle and was so appropriate to the white, dominant house on its hilltop. She found herself more entranced by the place as the days passed, one into another in brilliant weather such as she had never known before, a sheer blue sparkle to the Aegean that would have renewed hope in the heart of the most downcast person, and Fenny could never have said that she knew total gloom in the glory of the Grecian sun ... the accepted wife, after all, of Heraklion Mavrakis.

She discovered that Lion was a tireless worker, flying off some mornings in the Alouette and not returning for days at a time, his various business activities keeping him occupied in Athens or Cyprus, and occasionally in Istanbul.

Zonar often travelled with him, and the running of the island was in the capable, rather serious hands of Demetre.

He seemed intent on not accepting Fenny into the inner life of the family, but his wife proved to be a bored, fashionable, oddly pretty woman who found her new sister-in-law a source of curiosity. Adelina didn't offer her friendship, exactly, but she did prove to be more sociable than her husband. They had been married about five years and were childless. Adelina admitted to Fenny that she didn't care to go through the traumatic mess of childbearing, and Metre was too much in love with her to insist on his full quota of Grecian rights. 'This business of being a proud mother is overrated,' she said, in her languid voice. 'It ruins the figure and Greek men, believe me, transfer their attention to the children. Most of it!'

Fenny merely smiled and kept her own counsel. She knew her own secret fears, and Adelina was the last person in whom she meant to confide.

Zonar's little boy was a delight, but his nurse was rather possessive and even slightly hostile towards Fenny. She was a youngish woman and it occurred to Fenny that she might be in love with Zonar, who was a remarkably attractive man.

Life at the Blue Castle offered her a challenge rather than contentment, but she didn't mind that. She had decided not to be defeatist in the face of Lion's lack of love for her. There was always the remote possibility that he would soften towards her ... it was a straw in the wind, but she clung to it; if she let go of it there would be nothing but an empty abyss of a future into which she would fall, into the darkness out of the sun.

Here at the *kastello* she awoke to a wild beauty, the breath of lemons in the rampant green groves, the sunlight on the icon of the Virgin with hands reposed, and often to the sound of the helicopter drifting off into the blue heights, heading off with Lion, leaving her alone without a good-bye.

She had to accept his attitude and she did so with a gallant tilt to her chin, facing the day in the cool shantung so favoured by Penela and which certainly suited her own cool fairness.

After that first night on the island Lion took no more heed of her moods, as he probably thought of them, and he came and went in her bedroom as the whim took him. 'You are my wife,' he told her, with an iron firmness. 'I don't intend to treat you as a holy icon to be briefly kissed and set back in its cool white niche. You are a woman and you will learn to please me whether you want to or not.'

So, in spite of her secret fears, Fenny had to accept whatever the fates had in store for her ... she knew seven weeks after she had been at the Blue Castle that she was going to have Lion's baby, but she had no intention of confiding her news to him. She had made up her mind to keep to herself as long as possible the fact that he had already set her on the road away from him. She clung tightly, desperately, to the faint hope that he would one day forgive her and keep her with him. And for the sake of the tiny life growing within her slim body she absorbed all she could of the beauty of the island.

It was a landscape so dramatic that it gave rise to emotional thoughts and a kind of poetry of the senses. The fragrance of everything filled the air and stole into the pores of the skin in a subtle and disturbing way. And Fenny soon discovered why this island was called Petaloudes ... the branches of the trees quivered with the huge butterflies, their wings edged as if by lace. If a branch was disturbed, these lovely things flew into the air in a shaft of colour and lightness, the very air shimmering as if alive with gems.

The beauty of the scene would clutch at Fenny's heart and she would softly, wildly tell herself that it had all been worthwhile, to snatch a year of tempestuous living for herself ... a year she must turn into a lifetime.

Sandals in hand, and clad in a chiton-type dress that fluttered coolly about her limbs, Fenny made her way to the *yali* on its stone ledge just above the beach. This was a Turkish style summerhouse, furnished with small tables and a divan like one big cushion. The floor was covered by a woven carpet of many patterns and there were big pottery jars with frieze-like figures painted on them. There was comfort here, and solitude high above the sun-shot Aegean.

Fenny liked to come here when Lion was away, to play

records of *bouzoukia* music, to read the English magazines which he brought her from the mainland, and to watch the black peregrines and kestrels flying low over the water. Often she stayed until the dusk fell, and to the sound of Athene's owls she would go down to the cool beach with her hair tied to the crown of her head and she would swim alone, the sun having been drowned for the day and the air like wine from goblets of starry silver.

Aphrodite, she would think as she swam alone, renewing her chastity in the ocean ... if that were possible for a woman who knew that her body harboured the child of her lover.

She thought always of Lion as her lover, for he never behaved like a husband. He never confided his business concerns to her, nor his future plans. She was but an interlude in his life and he let her know it, whispering softly and tauntingly to her after making love to her, 'I may even miss this, my little fraud, when I send you away – to make a fool of some other man rich enough for your liking.'

She didn't argue with him, or protest; it was useless to do so, like pounding against a wall behind which she had been sealed like a guilty penitent.

He would come to her, stay a while, and then fly off to that other life in the busy cities, where another woman might be allowed to know him better than Fenny did.

For now, to swim like this in silvery water under the witchery of the stars, was an alleviation of the dull ache that sometimes grew into a very real agony, and then all at once she caught the sound of the helicopter chugging its way towards the plateau where the landing lights were always switched on in readiness for the return of the Alouette. It hovered above the sea, swinging in a graceful arc as it came gradually lower, and Fenny floated on her back and felt a jolt of surprise. She had not expected Lion back so soon, for Zonar had said that they were attending a conference in Cyprus.

The helicopter settled, and then fell into silence, and though she felt an irresistible urge to go and meet Lion, she stayed in the water and told herself that he wouldn't want to see her, running to him like any normal, loving wife. It was not her place to offer what she felt for him; he merely took if the mood for taking was upon him when he returned home from the pressures of his work.

Fenny was sitting alone on the deserted beach, hands clasped about her knees as she gazed at the rolling sea, when she caught the rattle of stones on the cliffside. She knew instantly that someone was coming down the path to the sands, and her heart quickened to the hope that it might be Lion actually seeking her out.

She went on looking at the water, for if it was Lion then she didn't want him to catch a glimpse of the eager expectancy in her eyes. If only it were he, wishful of wanting her just for herself ... her heart beat so fast that she felt a little faint and she had to take several deep breaths of the tangy air.

'*Kalispera, kyria*,' said a deep male voice, only it wasn't the gravelly tones of Lion that came from the tall figure crossing the beach in her direction. Her disappointment was deep and thrusting as a knife, and her fingernails dug themselves into her hands as she strove to turn to Zonar with a bright, friendly smile.

'Good evening, brother-in-law,' she said. 'You are back soon – have you come alone and left my husband at his desk?'

She expected Zonar to return her smile and to say something pleasantly insignificant. Instead he stood there looking down at her, and the bright reflection of the stars on the water showed Fenny the unusual sternness of his handsome face. She stared up at him and she had a sudden premonition of trouble.

'What is it?' She jumped to her feet and clutched at his sleeve. 'Has anything happened to Lion – you must tell me quickly or I'll go mad!'

'As bad as that with you, eh?' His black brows shaded his eyes and made him look very much like Lion. 'It would kill you to lose him?'

'God, yes!' She shook his arm, frantically. 'Don't be like him – don't torment me! Why are you back so soon?'

'There was an incident – for the love of heaven don't pass out!' He caught hold of her and the next minute had lifted her into his arms and was carrying her up the path to the *yali*. His shoulder thrust open the door and he carried her to the divan, laying her down with a gentleness she had never known from Lion. He stroked the damp hair away from her colourless face and he knelt there, looking down into her frightened eyes.

'An – incident?' she whispered. 'Has Lion been hurt?'

'Yes – and don't scream.' His hand pressed lightly against her lips. 'He's as tough as only a real Greek can be and the explosion merely knocked him out for a while, and the doctor had to dig some glass from his arm and his back. I had a luncheon appointment with – with someone, so I wasn't there at the Administration Building when the bomb exploded – Lion was one of the lucky ones, for some of the other men were killed and maimed.'

'Oh, God,' she said, shivering with reaction, 'why do these things have to happen? Why can't people behave in a civilized manner? It's barbaric, throwing bombs around – torturing each other because their politics don't happen to be the same. I must go to him—'

'He's all right, believe me. We brought him back in the

Alouette and now he is resting in his room. The doctors filled him with a drug which has made him sleepy – he will sleep and the shock will wear off.'

'I must see him – to make sure—' She was struggling to rise, but Zonar held her where she was, firmly and with a smile drifting into his dark eyes as he regarded her.

'He's all in one piece, I assure you, Fenella. Tomorrow he will be his usual commanding self, with no doubt a headache and his arm in white bandage to add to the attraction of the wounded warrior. You will then be able to make a fuss of him and insist that he follow the doctor's advice and rest a week from his infernal labours. By the gods, what other man would leave a lovely piece of woman all alone on an island like this one, to swim by herself in the Aegean and lie around in a Turkish *yali* like some neglected *fille de joie*? That,' said Zonar explosively, 'wasn't meant to be your fate!'

'It is my fate and I – I'm not complaining.' But her lips trembled as she spoke and her lashes fell concealing the look in her eyes. 'I'm only too grateful that Lion hasn't been horribly mutilated – you are telling me the truth, Zonar? He is all right, apart from lacerations?'

'I would never lie to you.' Zonar took her hand and brushed his lips across her fingertips. 'In some ways my hard-working brother deserves you, but in others he doesn't. He shouldn't neglect you—'

'Oh, he doesn't entirely do so.' Her lips moved in a half-smile. 'It's just that he needs his work far more than he needs me – I serve a purpose and I accept that he doesn't find complete happiness in my company. I'm not the one that he loves – it makes all the difference, you know that, and I wouldn't want him to pretend that he cares. It isn't part of Lion's character to wear false colours; he's totally direct in word and deed.'

'He's brutally honest, you mean.'

'I – I don't like that word – it doesn't apply.'

'No?' Zonar arched a black eyebrow. 'I have known Lion far longer than you, *kyria*, and I know how ruthless he can be with anyone who plays what he thinks of as an underhand game, especially with him as the opponent.'

'The game I played was underhand,' she said quietly. 'I don't expect Lion to treat me – fondly.'

'I don't like it that he treats you – unkindly.' Zonar's eyes stole over her slim figure in the flimsy swim-suit. 'You were meant to be loved by a man, not used to bring relaxation to the restlessly energetic mind and body of my brother, much as I respect the drive and courage of him. You have more to give than your lovely shape—'

'Zonar, please don't say such things—'

'It's about time they were said!'

'You're taking advantage of Lion's present helplessness and it isn't fair of you. I must go to him!'

'Not just yet.' He pressed her back against the divan cushions. 'You will hear me out and be told that you are worth a dozen of that showy cousin of yours. She gave me the eye, did you know that? The eye behind Lion's back! I could have spanked her backside for that!'

'He loves her, and there's no logic in love and there never will be. Let me go now, Zonar, before we both say things that we may regret.'

'I could never regret speaking with you – knowing you, Fenella.' His hands held hers and she felt the pressure of the large, dark-seal ring which he wore. 'Your strange and elusive charm is like nothing I have known before and I tell you this, you're wasted on a man who puts the conflicts of big business before the most exquisite pleasure in life – that of holding a woman in one's arms and sharing with her the total raptures of earth and heaven. They are there to be had within the compass of the arms, an end to the many terrors we must face when we're alone.'

He gazed down at Fenny and a wicked gleam came into his eyes. 'You look as if you could be divinely good, but instead you proved to be deliciously bad. Some men find it hard to forgive that what they judged to be an untouchable little nun turned out to be a naughty girl—'

'I'm not the kind of naughty girl you have in mind!' Fenny wrenched her hands from Zonar's and her eyes kindled into temper. 'You speak of your respect for Lion, and in the same breath you – you make a proposition to me! I'm shocked and disappointed in you. I thought you were nice.'

'Shocked?' He gave a little laugh. 'Because I find you charming and I would like to make you happy?'

'I'm happy enough – more than I deserve to be.'

'You truly believe that?' Zonar shook his head incredulously. 'I've sometimes watched you when you have been quite unaware of me, playing here on the beach like some lonely child, turning over the bits and pieces of sea-wrack and wiping the sand grains from the washed-up shells, and I have barely stopped myself from coming down to you. He leaves you too much alone! What you have is an enslavement, not a marriage!'

'It's for me to know what I have, Zonar, and you have no right to turn over my feelings as if – as if they were seashells.'

'I care for you and that gives me the right.' He leaned down to her and she gazed into the face of a weathered Adonis, strong and emotional, with a sensual cut to the lips and the classic chin. Above his night-dark eyes his hair was so black that he couldn't help but look the dangerously attractive man that he was.

Fenny's heart leapt nervously, for she was so alone in the summerhouse with him, and the ruthless Mavrakis streak ran in him and not far beneath the surface of his warm, tanned skin.

'As each day dies in the arms of night, so each woman should live in the arms of someone who truly cares,' he murmured. 'It's the fatal flaw in everyone that they must be loved.'

'I can survive without a *liaison dangereuse*,' Fenny rejoined. 'Lion would beat you for speaking to – to his wife like this.'

'Without a doubt,' he said casually. 'It wouldn't be the first time that he gave me a hiding. Did you imagine I was an easy youth for him to rear and educate?'

She smiled, reluctantly. 'You're a bit of a devil, Zonar. I like you and I'd hate anything to spoil our friendship. You don't really want an affair with me, you just feel cynically obliged to try it on with most of the women that you meet.'

'You are cynical to say that,' he reproved her. 'You know well enough that I find you beautiful and quiet – like a sea pool in the midst of the gritty sands of life. I envy Lion like hell! Especially if you love him!'

'I do.' The words came softly, from her heart itself. 'I think I always shall.'

'Despite the way he treats you?' Zonar frowned, and again his likeness to Lion was very apparent. 'In many ways Lion can be rough with people, for it was only Metre and I who had the benefit of a polished education that turned us from a pair of street Arabs into a couple of passable gentlemen. Lion worked in the marble quarries that he now owns, and helped build the *caiques* which carry his goods to a hundred foreign ports. God gave him his stamina and his business acumen, and I think the power of big business is all he really cares about. I think he admires a well-run ledger more than the shapely lines of a woman. And you say you love him!'

'Yes,' she said, and felt again that clutch of visceral terror that Lion could ever be less than vitally alive. She became poignantly aware of the tiny embryo deep within her body ... the slim body which Lion had possessed with those hands of his, scarred along the fingertips by the heavy work he had done in order to feed and clothe his young brothers.

'You owe him a great deal, Zonar. You should remember that.'

'I don't forget it,' he assured her. 'He's a great individual – subtle, unpredictable, partly masked and maddening. I'd kill for him!'

'Yet you—' Fenny bit her lip. 'You'd like to make love to me, his wife.'

'And be accursed for it, being a Greek whose brother's wife must be sacred.' He gave a wholly cynical smile, while deep in his eyes there lay a shadow. 'I'm drawn to you and I just can't help myself. You never intrude upon a man's thoughts – so quiet and deep, can I help it if I want to drop my soul into you?'

'Don't – please!'

'You are like the background music to a man's thoughts.'

'Zonar, your thoughts are not a symphony!'

'They are where you're concerned.'

'It's wicked music and you know it!'

'There's a certain delight to wicked things.' A smile curled around his well-cut lips. 'I wonder if my Aleko will take after me?'

'He's a delightful child,' she said warmly. 'You must be a good father for his sake.'

'Oh, Fenella,' he laughed and sighed together, 'there is a touch of the little nun hiding away in you, after all. By heaven, there's nothing more infuriating than a pretty woman in love with another man.'

'You're incorrigible,' she said, and this time she managed to evade him and rather thankfully she escaped from the *yali* and started up the path to the *kastello*. The sea wind blew her hair about her face and her lips were anxious, her eyes eager to see Lion and be reassured that he was all right. Zonar fell into step beside her, tall but without the same rugged power in his shoulders that made Lion stand out from other men. He walked lightly, easily, but without that hint of lithe, animal aggression that was so much a part of Fenny's husband.

Her husband ... lying hurt by a bomb so that she wanted to rush wildly to his side and throw herself across him. She felt the primitive urge run through her and she realized that no more was she entirely the self-restrained English girl. Something of Lion's pagan personality had entered into her and was running in her veins. He had made her his whether he loved her or not ... even if the future tore them apart she would be bound to him as if by a cord ... Andromeda tied to her rock.

When she and Zonar reached the brow of the cliffs they stood a moment looking down towards the starlit sea. It was then that she remembered she had left her dress behind in the summerhouse and was still clad in her swim-suit, with her feet bare and white against the soil. She dug her toes into the Greek soil and wished that she were planted here as firmly as a fig tree or one of the ancient olives whose roots ran deep into the earth and the rock.

'One seems to breathe the history of Greece off the very surface of the Aegean,' she said. 'So much legend and so much fact all woven in together so that one can hardly tell the truth from the fable. I find your land incredibly fascinating.'

'And the people?' he murmured, with that quirk of a smile at the edge of his lips. 'The Mavrakis clan in particular?'

'An arrogant lot,' she smiled. 'Almighty proud of themselves.'

'We have reason – from the gutter to a castle is no mean achievement. Looking at us now who would believe that we weren't part of the landed gentry?'

'Who indeed?' She looked at Zonar, standing there like a Greek god, but clad in a modern denim suit and a light brown button-down shirt, on his wrist a gold watch and on his hand a gleaming seal ring. 'It is only clothes that separate kings from beggars, isn't it, here in Greece? Your people have wonderful faces.'

'Why – thank you.' He seemed slightly embarrassed for a moment, as if her remark shook his usual self-assurance. 'I like you, too.'

'Zonar, don't get me wrong.' She began to walk on and he followed her, laughing. 'I find you handsome, but that doesn't mean that you make my knees go weak.'

'It takes Lion to do that, eh?'

'It takes love, and you know it!'

'I loved my wife, Fenella, but I can't make love to the dead. Do you think I should take to the weeds and self-denial of the widow? I couldn't for the life of me!'

'You could find yourself another nice girl to marry. Aleko needs a mother.'

'All the nice girls are already married to their brutal spouses. Why is it, I wonder, that niceness is attracted to hardness? You would find me a much more considerate lover.'

'Really? Do you keep your diplomas on the walls of your room, bearing their gold seal of feminine approval?'

'Why not come and see for yourself?' Now they had reached the stone garden that lay along the boundaries of the groves, where ruins and old rambling walls had been left as they were, on probably the site of an old pagan temple. Here as Fenny looked around her she caught the hooded gaze of stone gods, and saw the falling green stars of fireflies in the gloom.

'Zonar, may I have a promise from you?' she said.

'You may have whatever you wish, Fenella.' He held aloft a swathe of creeper and as she ducked beneath it, she saw his quizzically smiling eyes.

'I want your sincere promise that you'll treat me only as a friend, and as your sister-in-law. No more flirting.'

'Because you find it repellent, or because it's dangerous?'

'You know it's dangerous. I belong to your brother.'

'From the crown of your head to the soles of your feet, sister-in-law?'

'Yes.' She made her confession almost inaudibly, for Lion's possession of her was the most precious thing in her life.

'Go on like that and you will end up a little mother.'

Her heart thumped. 'Could I really?'

'It's a fact of marriage when a girl marries a Greek. Is that what you want above all?'

Oh no, not above all! How could she want her separation from Lion in the shape of his child? She pressed a hand to her abdomen, but the baby was there and she knew it in her very bones. Growing each day, so very much a part of her and only to remain hers if she voluntarily left Lion before he could take his son away from her.

Oh yes, she knew it was a son, for the Mavrakis brothers made sons in the shape of their darkly splendid, self-made selves.

'Come, lonely charmer, let me escort you into the castle.' Zonar lightly took her arm and she didn't pull away from him. Above all Lion had made gentlemen of his two brothers, and they knew he'd kill them if they ever broke his great trust in them. And she needed to enjoy idle, friendly talk with Zonar, for he didn't judge her.

'To a Greek,' he said, 'a son is the torch of life, burning on when his own flame goes out. It is no small thing to be the mother of a Greek child, and I'll make a bet that if you give Lion a son, he will forget that you ever played that little trick on him – if that's what you want.'

Forget? She shivered as they stepped into the hall of the *kastello*, where the great hammered lantern in the stairwell threw its jewel light down upon the white walls and archways.

'Run and change out of that brief piece of swimwear – run!' Zonar watched her as she started up the stairs. Suddenly she paused to turn and smile down at him, grateful that he found her congenial and was glad she was here.

'You're good for my morale,' she called down to him softly.

'But not for your morals, eh?' His smile was wickedly attractive as he stood there, an elk-sandalled foot upon the bottom stair, gazing up at Fenny and seeing only her, slim and pale-honey-skinned in her bathing-suit.

Neither Fenny nor Zonar noticed the appearance of the nursemaid from one of the rooms, prim and proper in her dark dress with its starched white collar.

'Sir!'

The sound of her voice came as a surprise, and both Fenny and Lion's brother looked almost guilty as they transferred their attention from each other to the figure of his son's nurse.

'I wished to speak with you regarding Aleko,' she said, looking directly at him and ignoring Fenny. 'He has been a little off his food – it may be due to this spell of very hot weather we've been having, but on the other hand—'

'On the other hand?' Zonar gave her a rather irritable look. 'It is your business to know about children. That is why you were hired.'

'Yes, sir.' The nurse stiffened and now her glance flashed up the stairs to where Fenny stood. 'I know *my* place in this household.'

With these words she retreated into the room from which she had appeared, and it struck Fenny that the nursemaid disliked her, and she might well have put a far from innocent interpretation upon that smile which had been exchanged between Zonar and herself. He was a good-looking widower in his early thirties, whose roving eye seemed to have passed over the nurse and not noticed that she was attracted to him.

Men could be cruel, as Fenny well knew, but there were women who could be spiteful in a far more destructive way. Her fingers clenched the wrought-iron balustrade of the stairs, and cold, invisible fingers seemed to run up and down her spine.

'Run along,' Zonar said. 'Go to your husband.'

She nodded and sped away from him, and his smile was thoughtful as he turned from the stairs and went towards the door through which the nurse had retreated.

When Fenny reached Lion's bedroom she was surprised to find the door ajar. She hastened inside and then came to an abrupt halt. Kassandra was standing beside the big bed, gazing down intently at the dark sleeping face against the white pillows.

'What are you doing?'

The woman turned instantly from the bed, and her face seemed more Byzantine than ever before, the nose etched in a straight line from her forehead, her hair blue-black against her skin that years of Greek sunshine had baked to a pagan darkness. A strange, tall woman whom

Fenny knew to wander in the moonlight, droning to herself. It was she who sometimes played the mandolin with such a magical touch; she had, so Lion had told Fenny, been tortured during the war for being a partisan who carried food and information to the Greeks who hid in the hills and fought the enemy in the dark.

'The *kyrios* is all right?' Fenny came swiftly to the bedside and gazed down at Lion with anxious eyes. Never before had she seen him like this, so deeply, helplessly asleep, his thick hair ruffled against the pillows, startling in its blackness against the white linen. His profile had a carved, shadowed look, and the lips were relaxed from their habitual stern line. One of his arms was outside the covers and it was bandaged from the wrist to the elbow.

'Oh, Lion!' Fenny gently stroked his hair, but he didn't stir. Zonar had said that he had been given a drug to make him sleep like this, but all the same it worried and frightened Fenny to see him so still, this man who was always so active, so restless, forever in need of something to keep him occupied.

She gave a start when Kassandra touched her on the arm and spoke in the Greek that Fenny was picking up with a rapidity which had even brought a compliment from Lion; a rather sardonic one, as if to remind her that her stay among Greeks was a limited one.

'The *kyrios* is strong,' said the Greek woman. 'I have seen his like in the war – lion-hearted, you say. He is well named.'

'He sleeps so deeply.' Fenny drew an anxious sigh. 'He seems so far away from us. I touch him and he doesn't even know.'

'It is good for him, *kyria*.' Kassandra smiled upon Fenny as if she were a child. 'He sleeps too little, does this man Mavrakis, driven day and night to provide bread for his family. That is because he starved as a boy, did you know that? He went hungry like a young dog so the other two could feed and grow. I knew him then. He found me for dead in a doorway and boy that he was he cared for me, and then fed me with the scraps that he begged, borrowed or stole. This one people love for more than the handsome face – you love him, no?'

Tears came flooding into Fenny's eyes and suddenly she broke down at Lion's bedside and wept from her very heart, her arms thrown across his hard legs under the covers. She cried brokenly, because he was alive, and because fate had not made her the woman that he wanted.

Kassandra patted her shoulder and left her to cry. 'But not too much,' she warned. 'For the sake of the child.'

The bedroom door closed behind her, and Fenny lay tense against the bed, her face wet with tears. So Kassandra knew! That strange woman had fathomed her secret... oh God, what if she told Lion!

Fenny knelt there beside the bed as the tears dried on her face, and she seemed unable to take her eyes from Lion's face. Never before had she seen the dark lashes so thick and still against the sun-darkened skin, those deep lines smoothed out a little from the sides of his fast-closed eyes. He breathed deeply and evenly, unstirring in his sleep, like a strong tree that had been felled for a while.

Even when he slept with Fenny, she had never awoken to find him beside her. He was always up and about almost at the crack of dawn, taking breakfast by himself, then off for a swim before working or flying away in the helicopter. How it had hurt that he should not need or want her company after spending part of the night with her, making her his and then disregarding her.

Yet none of it mattered... none of the hurt stopped her from loving him.

The room was very quiet except for the ticking of the

clock, the minutes slipping away as Fenny stayed there beside Lion, enjoying the luxury he never permitted when he was alertly himself. Never had she dared to let down her guard as she did right now, absorbing into her eyes every hard Greek line of his face ... the face she had so often longed to caress, stroking away those lines that the years of unrelenting work had carved into his skin.

And how strange to look at him and know that his eyes wouldn't suddenly open and find her own gaze so unveiled. The carved lids lay heavy in sleep, hiding the look that could disturb her in so many ways.

'Cold eyelids that hide like a jewel
Hard eyes that grow soft for an hour.'

With a sigh she arose from her knees and bending over him she very lightly brushed her lips across his cheek. He stirred slightly, and with her heart in her throat Fenny backed away from the bed ... was he going to wake up and find her standing here like a lovesick idiot? But as she watched him, tensed for flight, he settled back into the depths of his slumber and she took a breath of relief and made her way to her own bedroom.

Her young maid was there, laying out lingerie for her. From the open door of the bathroom there stole a scented mist of hot water. Fenny smiled at the girl. 'I've been sitting with my husband for a little while,' she said, speaking English which the girl understood. She had, before coming to work at the Mavrakis house, been employed by a woman writer. Her name was Anne (meaning mother in Turkish) and she was a dignified girl, with a soft skin and large dark eyes. When Lion had insisted that she have a maid, Fenny had been glad that he hadn't chosen for her some pert creature who would expect her to be a fashion-plate like Adelina. Fenny liked nice clothes, but she had never been all that interested in the rituals of make-up and coiffure. She liked to be as natural as possible.

'Will the *kyria* dress for dinner?' Anne inquired, turning from the deep cupboard where Fenny's dresses were hung. She had to think of them as hers, despite her constant awareness of Penela like a shadow between Lion and herself.

'No, I shall eat dinner on the *moussandra*,' she said. 'I couldn't face formal dinner with the family tonight.'

'Of course not, *hanim*.' The Turkish girl smiled gently and drew a long silk caftan from the cupboard. 'It was a great blessing that the *bey* was not badly injured, but a sadness that our peoples can't live in harmony.'

'Harmony,' Fenny said softly. 'What a lovely word that is, and what a hopeless dream. I don't really know what Lion *bey* was doing at the Administration Building in Cyprus, for he didn't tell me he was joining a conference there. I suppose, Anne, you wouldn't have heard any gossip among the staff?'

If the girl was surprised that Fenny shouldn't be in her husband's confidence, she didn't betray it. 'I did hear, *hanim*, that he had been elected to a rather important committee on the island of Cyprus. The people trust his sort far more than the men of politics; he has a reputation for being very fair and just.'

'So that's it?' Fenny murmured, going into the bathroom followed by Anne. 'I might have guessed. Do you think he has political ambitions?'

'Who can tell with men, *hanim*?' Anne smiled and took from Fenny the swim-suit as she stepped into the black marble bath, the water being let in through the nose and tail of a green dolphin. 'They insist that we women are a mystery to them, but it is often the other way about. Men will never truly believe that women are their equals of the mind; they prefer the idea of the *haremlik*, and in many ways it has a certain pleasantness.'

'Yes, it has.' Fenny sank back into the warm embrace of

the scented water. 'Deep down in themselves women don't really like to face the harsh facts of life, but they're inescapable, and the *haremlik* has a kind of romance about it. Does everyone think of me as the slave girl of the *bey*?'

'Does the *hanim* mind that they think so?' The girl soaped Fenny's back and shoulders with slim hands that looked brown against the pale-honey skin. 'He's much of a man, and tonight the people of Petaloudes will kiss their icons and offer thanks that he has been spared to them.'

'Will they really do that?' Fenny was deeply moved by the idea. 'Is he that important to them?'

'They depend on him for a livelihood, *hanim*.' The girl poured a fragrant oil from a small container and smoothed it over Fenny's skin, and she submitted almost like an infant. It felt nice to be cared for, and it was an added joy that Lion lay safe and sound in his bed. To these people she was his woman and that made her of some consequence — Lion's woman, shafting through her body a sensation of pure pleasure. How good the feeling was, and tonight she wouldn't spoil it by thinking of the future. She didn't dare to think that far ahead.

'Tell me, Anne, how does one give thanks like an islander? What do I have to do?'

'You take to the chapel something of gold or silver that you value and you give it away, *hanim*.'

'Thereby proving that worldly goods have no value beside the love of a human being?'

'That is so.' Anne held a large bath-towel, into which she folded Fenny as she stepped from the bath.

'The chapel is on the hillside above the village, isn't it?'

'Yes, *hanim*, but you are not going there tonight? Your husband would be displeased—'

'No, I shall go tomorrow morning. I'll go early and take

the small car.' As Fenny slipped into her caftan she was wondering what she had to give of gold or silver ... all she really had of great material value was the chain of pearls which Lion had put around her neck on their wedding night ... and the Aphrodite bracelet of gold which he had dropped into her lap the morning after that night.

She would have to give away the bracelet, for the pearls meant nothing to her. She never wore them. They lay always in their velvet case – Penela's pearls. But the bracelet – a quiver of pain ran across her face – that she loved and often wore in the evenings.

'What I give must have personal value only?' she asked Anne, who now stood behind her applying a brush to her hair and making it gleam in the lamplight. 'Must it be something that I like very much to wear?'

'I don't think that the *kyria* need to be too rigid in the matter.' Anne smiled into the mirror at Fenny's pensive face. 'The greater the material value of the offering the more use the good priest can make of the money.'

'That's a relief, and of course it's true. My pearls will make a very practical offering.' Fenny broke into a smile and felt not the slightest reluctance at parting with the chain of milky gems that just didn't have for her the charm of the bracelet, which one day might be all she had, apart from memories, to link her to Lion. She would never love anyone else. She would reach out, always, to touch him through the distance and she would never be able to reach him.

'Thank you, Anne,' she said. 'You can leave me now, and I'll have my supper out under the stars.'

'Have a good hour, *hanim*.' The young maid left her and quietly closed the door, leaving Fenny all alone.

She sat there for a moment or two, and then opened the drawer in which she kept her trinkets and took out the Aphrodite bracelet. She put it on her arm, liking the feel of it, almost like warm, tawny fingers against her skin.

Oh God – she pressed her face into her hands and there rushed over her that awful cold terror of the future. She wasn't like Penela, or other girls she had known. She would never love like this again, and there was nothing ... nothing beyond the precarious happiness of these months with Lion.

CHAPTER SIX

A TABLE was laid for her out on the *moussandra*, the white lace cloth glimmering in the restful light of a wall lantern, with a glint of silver cutlery and the softness of flowers in a small vase.

She enjoyed an excellent meal of *moussaka*, which was a delicious pie made of layered aubergine, minced meat, cheese, tomato and egg, served with little onions no bigger than the top of a man's thumb. With it she had a glass of red wine, not too sweet, and a dessert of caramel pudding with grated nuts.

The night air of Petaloudes blew softly over the parapet of the little room, spiced with the many flavours between fig, pine and an ocean deep with stars. Though alone Fenny didn't feel lonely ... that peculiar torment lay beyond the pagan seas that came shifting and shining against the cliff walls of the *kastello*.

When she had finished eating she went to stand at the parapet with a second glass of wine (why not?) clad in her long silk robe and embroidered slippers, her hair shining and Alice-like down the straight line of her spine. It was there that she was unexpectedly joined by Adelina, who wore a pleated shirt in pure white silk and a long red skirt. Her glossy dark hair was worn away from her face, which always struck Fenny as being like a golden mask in which gleamed narrow dark eyes and scarlet lips. She was like a living effigy off an Egyptian tomb – Kat the goddess.

Upon first meeting Demetre's wife, Fenny had thought that she would be supercilious and even a little biting. But Adelina had a capricious sense of humour that made even her most edged remarks amusing rather than deliberately cruel.

That she was totally dedicated to herself she never bothered to hide, but Demetre so obviously adored her that Fenny realized it was a waste of time to feel sorry for him.

Love was a curious emotion. It took no heed, as she had found out, of the pain it mixed with its pleasure.

'Zonar said you were dining in lonely splendour, but all the same I came to keep you company for a while. Is that all right? I shan't bother you, eh?' Adelina came forward with her feline walk, a cigarette in a jade holder. 'So the Lion has had some of his tawny pelt damaged. One thing you can say, you do live dangerously.'

'Do I?' Fenny was always a little on her guard with Adelina, whose self-devotion could never make her vulnerable. She enjoyed being an object of love and desire, but it just didn't occur to her to return the compliment. The worries and anxieties of love, she said, caused lines in the face and she didn't intend to encourage any of those.

'Lion Mavrakis is a dangerous man, is he not?' Adelina raised her jade holder and let a stream of smoke waft from her fine-wrought nostrils. 'Exciting, of course, but as difficult to control as any creature of the jungle. I know where I am with Metre. He has the looks without the menace. Metre doesn't mind that I have no intention of making him a father, but your personal life with Lion must be – well, to say the least, an overwhelming experience. I bet he doesn't admit the word "no" into his vocabulary.'

Fenny merely quirked her lips against the rim of her wine glass, for she had no intention of discussing her personal life with Lion.

'Certain English women can be so maddening in their reticence.' Adelina's smile was narrow as her eyes flicked over Fenny, taking in the gold sheath of hair down over the silk of her caftan, and the pallor of her throat against the amber silk. 'You have a certain beauty and I should feel envious of you – I probably would if Metre gave you the eye as Zonar does.'

Fenny stirred against the parapet and felt the quickening of the pulse in her neck. 'Zonar is intrigued by most women,' she said. 'It means nothing—'

'It had better mean nothing, dear. Lion is a generous devil, but he draws the line at sharing his women, even with a brother, and Greek family feeling is probably the strongest in the world. How do you like being a member of a Greek dynasty, even a self-made one?'

'It has a fascination to it,' Fenny said, while all around in the softly rustling trees the numerous cicadas were filling the night air with their uneven chorus. 'And a kind of pride.'

'And don't forget the passion, dear.' Adelina gave a throaty little laugh. 'The trouble with Greeks is that when love awakes in them it's with a passion that can be merciless. They are better keeping to the arranged marriage – mine to Metre was arranged, you know, between Lion and my family. I brought a dowry with me and that makes me almost an independent woman – unlike you.'

The slim fingers of Fenny's hand clenched on the stem of her wine glass. It was true. All she had brought to Petaloudes was her love for Lion, and he didn't care a fig for her feelings; it was her body that aroused the primitive Greek in him.

'The arranged marriage strikes me as a very passionless business,' she said. 'What happens if a girl has no dowry?'

'Then she is condemned to being a spinster, or some married man's back-door woman. Greece in many ways can be a hard country, and it certainly takes nerve for a foreign girl to marry a Greek. Especially a girl like you.'

'Like me?' Fenny kept her gaze fixed upon the dark depths of the garden far below the railing of the *moussandra*. 'Yes, I rather asked for a complicated life, didn't I?'

'It's like a Greek drama,' Adeline laughed. 'Of course, it's strictly a family secret, and it didn't take me long to wheedle it out of Metre. Is Lion still smitten with the other girl – your cousin, eh?'

'As you said,' Fenny swallowed dryly, 'when a Greek falls in love he does it thoroughly, or not at all.'

'And what of an English woman when she falls in love?' Adelina stared curiously at Fenny, running her gaze up and down the delicate modelling of her profile. 'You are in love with him, are you not? You couldn't do what you did – he might well have broken your neck, if it hadn't been part of an attractive figure. Poor you! Your only dowry your body.'

Put into words it made a hard tremor shake through Fenny. It was a harsh truth that plunged into her like a knife.

'Oh, come,' Adelina drawled, 'it isn't so bad. You don't have to feel ashamed—'

'I don't,' Fenny said, almost fiercely. 'I don't cheat Lion in any way, so I can never suffer self-reproach no matter what else I – suffer.'

'One would take you for a Greek woman the way you dwell on self-sacrifice,' Adelina drawled. 'Thank heaven I don't have this urge to give all for the sake of love. You are young and attractive, yet already being in love has caused anguish for you. Be like me! Take a page from my book and be less of a giver and more of a taker. Men expect it, don't you know that? Angels make them feel uncomfortable.'

Fenny had to smile at the vision of Lion ever being put out of countenance by a woman. 'Lion takes me for a consummate actress right now,' she said. 'If I tried acting like you, Adelina, he would presume that I was trying for an Oscar.'

'An – Oscar?' Adelina looked puzzled. 'What is that?'

'An award for a good performance given to a film star.'

'Ah, I see. So my brother-in-law thinks you are only playing at being his loving wife? Why does he think you married him?'

'To be – well off. I lived in my uncle's house and I was the poor relation. For Lion all shades are densely black or pure white, like the effect the Greek sunshine has on things, creating those sable shadows against pallid walls.'

'Lion has made up his mind about you, eh? Well, if he thinks you mercenary, then you must take advantage of his estimate of you. Tell him you need some new clothes and you and I will fly to the mainland one day soon and I will take you to see Constantine, my dressmaker in Athens. He's very clever and Lion can certainly afford to let him dress you. What do you say?'

'I'd very much like a trip to Athens.' Fenny was so relieved by the change of topic that she sounded more eager than she felt. 'I'm not all that clothes-conscious, but it would be fun to visit the Greek capital.'

'There is no other quite like it. I might even endure a climb to the Acropolis so that you could take a look at the temple ruins of the Parthenon. The temple was dedicated to the virgin goddess of wisdom and valour, Athena, and is at its best by moonlight when the Ionic columns and the statues actually look white. During the day it's rather dusty and grey, with so many tourists bumping into each other with their cameras. I am sure they take more pictures of each other than the celebrated ruins.'

'Have you ever been to London?' Fenny asked, recalling that Adelina had not been with Demetre for the wedding that should have taken place between Lion and her cousin. With a reminiscent shiver she sank down into one of the cane chairs with a cushioned backrest. She placed her wine glass on the little table and felt the ache in her fingers from the way she had clenched the stem. If only she could be like her sister-in-law, leaning there against the parapet with all the relaxation of a cat; unconcerned that she return affection with anything more than the occasional purr.

'I prefer Paris,' she replied. 'I confess to one driving passion, and that is my love of clothes. It is a good thing I have an independent income from my father, who is in shipping, otherwise I should soon make a poor man of Metre. Does it puzzle you that I should marry him?'

'Not really.' Fenny leaned her head against the cushioning of her chair and willed herself to relax. 'He adores you and regards you as someone very special. How could you resist him?'

'Yes, it is nice to be a goddess in the eyes of a man.' A smile curved on Adelina's scarlet lips and she studied the gemmed bracelet on her wrist. 'Do you envy me?'

Fenny considered the question and let herself wonder what it might feel like to have Lion at her feet ... it was something impossible to imagine. There was too much pride in him, and far too much virility. He would never place any woman on a pedestal, and Fenny knew that she would far sooner be in his arms than out of his reach.

'No, you and I are very different kinds of women,' Adelina said shrewdly. 'You need the physical expression of a man's passion, but I am quite happy to be admired. I just don't regard it as the supreme peak of womanhood to go all out of shape for a man merely in order to go through the sweating discomfort of bearing his child. But you will want that, eh? And I don't doubt that Lion will demand it.'

Adelina swung from the parapet and gave Fenny a searching look. 'You have been looking rather fragile in the face just recently – are you in an interesting condition?'

'No.' Fenny made the denial involuntarily, for she couldn't trust Adelina not to tell Demetre if she admitted to being with Lion's child. She didn't want him to know just yet ... she shrank physically from what she would see in his eyes when they dwelt on her pregnant body. She would see there not love for the wife who carried his baby, but the triumph of a man revenged.

This child wasn't going to hold them together ... this tiny life that fed from her love was going to tear them apart.

'You sound very sure,' Adelina drawled. 'So the little interesting shadows under your cheekbones mean nothing? You certainly aren't dieting, from the look of those empty plates!'

'It's probably the heat that has caused me to lose some weight. We don't have this kind of weather in England, not for weeks on end.'

'Brrr, I couldn't live in a cold country.' Adelina stretched with sensuous pleasure in the silk against her skin, and the spicy scents of the Greek night. 'I need my visits to the fashion houses, but I like living on this island.'

'One of its exotic butterflies,' Fenny smiled.

'I like that description, dear. Well, I will leave you to your bridal reflections. I am happy that Lion came out of the fracas almost unscathed – *kalenikta*.'

Adelina strolled away, humming a little Greek tune to herself and perfectly content with her life on Petaloudes. Fenny sat on alone until a chill crept into the air, and very quietly she went into Lion's room to assure herself that he was all right. A ruby-shaded *lampada* was softly alight in a niche facing his bed, and it came as a shock when she leaned over him and found him looking into her eyes.

'Lion ...oh!'

'Hullo,' he said. 'I feel as if time had lagged. How long have I been asleep?'

'Hours.' She could feel her heart hammering away as she looked down into his eyes, curiously like velvet in the ruby shadows. 'How are you?'

'A trifle unlike myself. All I remember is a vivid flash and a blow on the head. What happened?'

'A terrorist set off a bomb in the building where you were. You were very fortunate—'

'You mean others were killed! What of Zonar?'

'He was out to lunch at the time of the explosion—'

'Of course, now I remember. He said he was seeing a college friend, but I suspect it was a girl.' Lion's teeth showed in a slight smile, and then his eyes clouded. 'It's an irony that men should die while trying to bring some sort of peace to Cyprus. So I was flown home, eh? And put to bed like a baby. That has never happened before!'

'Are you hungry?' She smiled to ever think that he could be a baby. 'It has been hours and it won't hurt you to eat something that you fancy.'

'How concerned and wifely you sound. Have your emotions been wrung, my darling?'

'Don't be unkind!'

'Ah, those eyes, what hurt they can express.' His fingers

slid beneath the full sleeve of her caftan and pressed against her skin. 'Soft and sweetly smiling as some pseudo-angel, aren't you? Come, it must have been a little of a disappointment when my brother had to tell you that you weren't a widow. Such a pity! How ravishing you would look in black chiffon – how effective against that skin of yours, and that hair.'

'Lion, you are a beast, but I refuse to lose my temper with you. Are you in need of some food?'

'*Kaffes tourkikos,* my ministering angel. Dark crusty bread and a dish of hot buttery snails.' His smile was wholly wicked. 'Cooked in herbs and vinegar-oil.'

'You shall have them – oh, Lion, you're indestructible, and everyone is so glad about it.'

'Are you?'

'I marvel at your *zoikos*. Snails and Turkish coffee at this time of night!'

'You asked my fancy, *guzel*.'

Her heart felt as if it jarred in her side. 'Flatterer! I'll go and cook those snails.'

'You?'

'Yes, I'm not just a rag and a bone and a hank of hair, you know. I once took a cookery course to augment the boredom of Wimbledon Common and having no dog to walk. My uncle wouldn't have an animal in the house. Hairs on the chairs, you know.'

'So you craved a dog, eh?'

'And I got a Lion.' As he sat up in bed she adjusted the pillows behind him, seeing the naked power of his shoulders and the whiteness of the bandage against his skin. 'I shan't be long – your arm, is it terribly sore?'

'Bearable. You don't have to bother with snails, *kyria*. A sandwich will suffice.'

'You will have exactly what you fancy, *kyrie*.'

'Being sentimental over my few scratches and my sore

144

head?' he mocked her. 'Don't forget the coffee, will you?'

'No, sir.' He was reaching for his cheroots when she left him, to run lightly downstairs in the direction of the big kitchen. During the day she was out of bounds in that domain of the Greek cook, but right now all was quiet there and the lights were out. Fenny turned them on and padded in her slippers to the immense ice-box, the folds of her caftan rustling silkily about her bare legs. There were always snails on ice because Lion was fond of them, and she quickly set about preparing a dozen for him, wrinkling her nose at the look of them. They bubbled away in the saucepan while she made the dressing for them and brewed the coffee. She sliced bread and placed a dish of butter on the table.

She was in the midst of her cookery when a tall figure suddenly stood in the open doorway of the kitchen. 'Feeling peckish?' drawled a voice.

She glanced up from the table and smiled at Zonar. 'Lion is awake and he's the one who is feeling peckish. He fancies snails, and I'd whip up a four-course dinner if he wanted it. It's marvellous to see him his old self again.'

'I bet it is!' Zonar lounged there looking quizzical. 'Has he insulted you yet?'

'About three times.'

'So he really is back on form?'

'Just about.' She dished up the snails and filled the kitchen with their aroma as she poured on the sauce, with its slight dash of garlic. 'If he's in pain he wouldn't say so.'

'You mean he prefers to eat snails rather than rest his sore head on your bosom?' Zonar's eyes ran over her. 'I know what I'd prefer of those two occupations.'

'He's feeling hungry and his strength has to be built up.' She placed the snail fork on the tray along with a snowy napkin and the thinly cut slices of crusty bread. As she added the pats of butter and the pepper she smiled to herself. It had felt good to be cooking for Lion and she only wished she could do it more often, but she just wasn't in a position to upset the routine of the *kastello*. The Greek cook would be most put out if she started using his kitchen, and Lion would be bound to say that he didn't pay wages to a professional in order to have the work performed by a novice.

'You can bring the coffee pot,' she told Zonar, 'and come and say something nice to your brother.'

'My dear sister-in-law, he would fall out of bed if I dared to tell him to his face that I'm hellishly glad he's still here to keep the lot of us on our toes.' Zonar followed her up the stairs, the long-spouted brass pot held by him with some amusement. 'I feel like a Greek waiter, taking up coffee like this.'

'It won't hurt you to make yourself useful,' she said, 'and don't you dare upset Lion.'

'My dear girl, he's the king of this jungle and I am merely one of the cubs he slaps down.' He laughed and followed her into his brother's bedroom. 'Here we are, Lion, at your service with just about the most tasty dish you will get in your life.'

'The snails or my wife?' Lion gave his brother a keen look, before glancing at Fenny as she placed the legged tray across his knees. 'They smell appetizing.'

'I hope you'll find them so. Are you comfortable, *kyrie*?'

'Fine.' He lifted the lid from his supper dish and his nostrils tautened hungrily. He took up the fork and expertly removed a snail from its shell, dipped it in the sauce and carried it to his mouth. As he chewed he slowly raised his eyebrows. 'Just the exact amount of garlic – amazing.'

'Oh, she isn't just a sweet face,' Zonar drawled, his long frame sprawled out in an armchair as he watched his brother ploughing into his supper with frank appetite. 'I can see, Lion, that you are feeling a lot better. It was a close shave, brother. Several of the committee didn't survive.'

Fenny quietly slipped away from the bedroom, leaving Lion and his brother to talk together, a soft prayer in her heart that her husband was safe in his king-size bed and not among those who lay cold and unknowing of any more delights. She knew that Lion was compassionate for their sakes, but he was human and alive, and it gave her a glow that the food she had cooked was exactly to his liking.

She went to bed in her own room and fell asleep to the murmur of deep voices in the adjoining apartment.

Daylight was stabbing in through the windows when she awoke, so bright and sun-filled that she realized at once that she had slept deeply and awoken rather later than usual. Lion! He came instantly into her mind and she scrambled out of bed and was only half-way into her robe as she entered his bedroom.

The great bed was empty, the covers thrown aside and the pillows dented from his head. Oh no! He should still be resting.

'*Kalimera, kyria.*'

She swung round and there he was, standing tall in the opening of the balcony doors, giving her a skin-teasing look which she just couldn't escape. 'Come over here and let me show you something,' he invited.

'Lion, why don't you have another day in bed?' she said. 'The doctor did advise you to take things easy—'

'I plan to. Come!' He held out a hand to her and out of sheer habit she went obediently to him and felt his fingers close hard around hers. He drew her out on to the balcony into the sunlight and directed her attention to the glittering sea. There on the blue-green water rode a beautiful black *caique*, looking like the raiding ship of some pirate who had decided to pillage the island, where indeed there were coves along the shore where in the old maurauding days the islanders had hid their young girls in the hope of keeping them safe from piratical attentions.

The setting was perfect, there beyond the ochre-pointed rocks and the sea rippling like silk. The sails of the *caique* were spread dark and silky against the speckless sky.

'There is the *Cyrene*,' he said. 'Only just out of the shipyard and ready for her first voyage. Do you like her?'

'Yours?' she breathed. 'I – I've never seen a ship so picturesque, so piratical. Yes, she could only belong to you, *kyrie*.'

'And do you fancy to go sailing in her on the Aegean?'

She heard him, but the words were too wonderful to believe in. It couldn't really be true that Lion was asking her to sail away with him somewhere ... anywhere ... heaven.

'Aren't you a good sailor?' he asked.

'I don't really know – I've never been put to the test.' She wanted to believe in the reality of such a voyage, out there on that fabulous ocean in that handsome *caique* with its great sails and its carved figurehead that would be the goddess Cyrene. The morning sea was shimmering around her in peacock hues, and there would be so many small Greek islands to be explored. She wanted it desperately, but once before she had wanted something with all her heart and when she had dared to reach for it there had been scorn in Lion's eyes and he had told her, in a voice like iron, that she could give him a child and then get out of his life.

She couldn't go sailing with him . . . she couldn't enjoy the heaven of it knowing all the time that the days and nights led inevitably to nowhere.

'You will be put to the test,' he told her. 'I've arranged for the *Cyrene* to pick us up later this morning.'

And then he looked away from his ship to Fenny's face and at once a tempered glint came into his eyes. 'Why are you looking like that?' he demanded. 'Aren't you keen to be alone with me on the *caique*? Don't the wifely attentions of last night extend to a sailing trip? Come on, if you don't welcome the idea then say so. I'm not so driven for company that I shall drag you aboard against your will, like one of those Turkish corsairs who used to plague these islands in the old days. Of course, it was inevitable that their blood should get into Greek veins, but as I have just said, I'm not that hard up for you. I never have been! We both know that, don't we?'

'Yes—' She pulled away as far as his hands would allow and at once his fingers tightened until she felt her bones would snap. 'You can take Zonar with you—'

'Take a brother?' He arched a brow and his mouth twisted. 'My dear, do you imagine you are the only woman in my life? If you don't fancy the trip, then rest assured that I can soon fill your berth with someone a little more eager. I suppose the disappointment of yesterday has now struck you – I came so close, didn't I, to making you a free woman, and a wealthy one at that.'

Fenny flinched as if he had struck her right across the face. 'I'll do whatever you say, Lion. I'll come sailing if you want that—'

'Go to hell!' He gave her a sudden push that sent her sprawling against the ironwork of the balcony, where she struck her rib cage and gave a gasp of pain. She clung there a shocked moment, staring at him as he stood like sculpture in the burning sunlight, dark and still, the bandage glaring white against the vigour of his forearm.

'You're hard as steel, Lion,' she panted. 'Y-you just don't want to understand me and so you put cruel interpretations upon all my motives. Nothing ... nothing changes you, not even a brush with death!'

'Right!' he said, his teeth a white, angry bar. 'Why should anything change me or my opinion of you? We are exactly where we were on the day you forced your way into my life. Nothing has changed, and now if you don't mind get out of my sight – by the Virgin, playing the angel of concern for my brother last night! Acting the little wife and hiding your chagrin behind that sweet, false smile that comes so readily to your lips. Thanks be I don't have to see you for the next ten days – I shall put miles of ocean between us and wish to heaven it could be final.'

'Don't think I'm not wishing the same.' She turned away on trembling legs and left him, a hand clenched against the pain in her side. In her room she sat frozenly on the bedside and realized the awfulness of the gulf which had opened between Lion and herself. With the dramatic suddenness of an earthquake it had happened; a disastrous moment of hesitation between the heaven of being with him on his beautiful ship, and the aftermath of being alone without him. She rocked back and forth in her distress and a little moaning sound came from her throat, of which she was quite unaware. She ached as if he had taken hold of her and thrown her over the balcony.

She would go away!

The resolve came suddenly and she knew she would keep it. He had said he would be gone for ten days, which should give her ample time to arrange her departure from

Petaloudes. She would hire a boat to take her across to Athens and from there she would book an air flight to England. She had savings in a bank there; sufficient money to see her through until the baby was born; then like many another woman she would find a job and support the baby on her own. She wasn't afraid. That way at least she would keep something far more precious than a gold bracelet.

She pressed her hand into her side and pain quivered across her face. Thank God no one knew that she was carrying Lion's child. There was only Kassandra, and she wasn't a member of the family and hardly likely to speak of it. She had only been guessing, anyway. And Fenny was a foreign girl whom no one would really miss.

She would quietly vanish out of the lives of the Mavrakis family and settle in some part of England where she would be anonymous.

Also this morning she would slip away from the *kastello* and by the time she returned from her trip to the chapel in the hills, Lion would be away on the *Cyrene*, sailing off in high anger, quite convinced that she was a mercenary little cheat. What a painful irony, when the only thing she wanted from him was the love he kept locked up with an iron key!

She would be cheating him when she left the island, taking with her the son he would never see. It had to be that way, for she couldn't take any more of this life that swung between passion and torment, with none of the tenderness to make bearable the hurts that a strong and tempestuous man could inflict.

This morning he had been physically violent for the first time, and when Fenny went into the bathroom to take a shower she found a bruise on her side. In his temper he might not have realized how hard had been the thrust of his hand, throwing her against the ironwork, and she was struck by a frightened coldness in the very pit of her stomach. Lion must hate her very much, and the only recompense she could make for forcing her way into his life was to disappear out of it.

She rang down for breakfast in her room, and afterwards dressed in a simple white dress enlivened only by the gold of her bracelet. She quietly made her way downstairs, carrying in her handbag the jewel-case that held the pearls. This trip to the chapel, there to offer a prayer and the pearls, was now a valid excuse to get away from the *kastello* for a few hours; by the time she returned Lion would have gone. There would be no goodbyes. No *kali andamosi*. She wouldn't have a kiss to remember him by, but a painful blow from his hand.

There was no one about as she made her way to the garage, where several cars were kept for the use of the family. The keys were in the ignition of the red two-seater and Fenny backed it out of the garage and swung the car to face the sloping driveway to the gates. The sun had now grown really hot, striking into the open vehicle and across the top of Fenny's head. She flinched and felt as if a needle were being driven into her temple; she should have thought to wear a hat, but all thought this morning was concentrated upon that scene with her husband. It was a kind of nightmare moment that wouldn't let go of her emotions. It was like being stabbed, having happened so quickly that only the torn feeling made it real.

She drove down towards the gates, standing open and wide to the corkscrew road that cut its way above the sea to the village. Although Fenny had never owned a car of her own the estate office for which she had worked had liked its staff to be able to drive so they could take prospective buyers in the firm's car to view property. In consequence of this she was a competent driver and felt no fear of the narrow and unpredictable road with its sudden swerves that offered direct glimpses of the ocean, and at one bend the sudden shattering sight of the *Cyrene* out there on the dazzling water.

Fenny caught her breath at the silhouette of the *caique* against the sun-fired sky. It was unreal in its proud black beauty, like a painting on canvas.

She stopped the car so that it seemed to hang precariously on that bend of the road and she gazed at the *caique* until her eyes were hazy and that needle-point of pain in her very brain. Had she been in control of that moment when she had deliberately ended what had been between Lion and herself? Or had fate decided that it should happen then, wiping the smile from his eyes and turning them to hard golden stone ... stone with a fire at its centre, as in a volcano, seething upwards out of the core of him, giving way to a fury that made him strike her!

Her hands clenched the wheel of the car. 'Go with God, my lion,' she murmured. 'I loved you more than you ever cared to know.'

She drove on, past the wild fig trees and the twisted olives that grew on the sloping borders of the road. The occasional goat clambered there, where shepherd tracks led away into the barren hills. The cliffs plunged downwards to sea-battered coves and soft white sand. The air was alive with a radiance of colour and the eternal creaking of the cicadas. Butterflies locked wings in the air, the males carrying a musk that attracted the females to them, vivid flights of courtship among the irises, the spineless white caper, and the pale blue devil in the bush.

Fenny drove into the village at the tails of a flock of goats and a thin brown youth in pantaloons. They had a dog with them and it ran at the side of the car, barking and snapping its pointed teeth at her. She knew these dogs to be rather wild and was glad she wasn't on foot.

The chapel gleamed white in the sun, dominating the small houses that sloped up the hillside, their ochre roof-tiles shading one another. She saw women busily spinning the great balls of raw wool at the doorways of their houses, their faces sun-baked and oriental. There was shadow and mystery beyond the oval archways of thick white stone and the grilles of ornamental stonework where creepers tumbled, their thick stems dark and bent against the sun-blistered walls.

Fenny parked the car near the courtyard of the chapel with its single belfry, a sleepy little building standing there green-shaded by tall cypress trees and several chaste trees with spiky blue flowers – Monk's Pepper, the trees that were supposed to subdue the passions.

At the entrance of the chapel there was a floor mosaic in a key pattern – welcome to friend and stranger alike, and Fenny stepped into the dim coolness and walked down past the figures of black-clad women sitting there absorbing some of the peacefulness before facing the chores and worries of the day. Soft light filtered in through oval windows filled with panes of coloured glass, and Fenny went forward to light a candle and lay in the offering plate the glimmering pearls that were too much a reminder that she was Lion's false bride and not the girl he had wanted to marry.

She knelt there in one of the pews and eyes closed, head bowed, she prayed for the strength to leave the man she loved too much to be able to endure any more his lack of love for her.

When she left the chapel she walked beneath the chaste trees, a solitary figure in white at which the village women cast glances of curiosity. They could see she was a foreigner and some of them might have guessed who she was. One or two wore visored scarves that gave them the look of orientals. They were people deep-rooted in the traditions of their past, and England seemed many miles away with its modern way of life.

Fenny breathed the spicy scents of the trees and saw the dance of yellow-winged butterflies, and she knew how passionate had been her hope that she could have become an islander like these people, putting down roots here and rearing a family for Lion.

But it wasn't to be ... their marriage had roots of clay, and she must leave all the wild and pagan beauty of this place, quietly saying *adio* as she walked in the village, past the bakery with its hot fragrant smell of fresh-baked bread, and the grocery store with its pungent aromas of dried fruit, honey and herbs. She saw an old Turkish fountain affixed to a wall, no longer used by the villagers for their drinking and washing, for water-pipes had been paid for by Lion and laid so that each house had this luxury that in modern cities was so taken for granted.

She strolled along by sea-walls built of big cobbles and saw the colourful fishing-boats with painted symbols on their sides, and it was there that she came upon a little *patisserie* with one or two tables set out on a pavement. She sat down at a table and when the moustached waiter came out to her, an enormous white apron to his boots into which black pantaloons were tucked, she smiled and ordered a water-ice. He then rattled off an assortment of flavours in passable English, and it turned out that he had once worked in a Greek restaurant in London, quite close to what he referred to as the tall glass tower of the telephone company.

'But I miss my peoples,' he said, his teeth flashing white as he placed an orange water-ice in front of Fenny. 'There is too much the rush and tear in London, but I saved my money and came home to make my own business. Will the *kyria* not try an egg-doughnut or a cream pastry? My wife she is very good with the making of cakes – Greek peoples very fond of nice cakes.'

It was so nice to see a friendly face that Fenny agreed to try an egg-doughnut, and she stayed talking with the owner of the *patisserie* for about an hour, and it wasn't until she was leaving that he asked her solemnly to give his very good wishes to the Kyrios Mavrakis and to say what a great relief it was that his injuries were not serious.

Fenny couldn't reply that she wouldn't be seeing her husband ever again, and so with a smile that shook a little on her lips she promised to pass on his good wishes.

'It is good that the *kyrios* has a kind and pretty wife.' The Greek bowed to her. 'May you go with happiness, *kyria*.'

'*Evkharisto*,' she said, and knew that she would go with sadness, and as she walked away the sea blurred as tears came into her eyes.

About ten minutes later she was driving away from the village, past an old windmill on a hill, its twelve small sails circling lazily in the warm air. Its roof was thatched, its walls a crusty white, and it looked so picturesque that Fenny turned a moment from the wheel to glance back at the windmill. And it was in that instant that one of the goatherding dogs dashed out from undergrowth and ran barking in front of the car. Fenny wrenched at the wheel and trod down hard on the brake in order to avoid the animal – the car lurched towards the cliffside and she felt rather than heard a grinding sensation beneath her foot. The car scraped the cliff wall, then came back on the road with a jolt, facing the slope that ran downwards until it curved on to the next section of narrow highway.

The car sped down that slope and suddenly for Fenny there was no way of stopping it. Something had happened to the brakes and they were as limp and useless as a broken bone. The vehicle raced towards that curve and

Fenny held on grimly to the wheel, just managing to turn on that sheer bend, at such an angle that the cliffs again reared in front of her, the colour of fire and jade in the sunshine that poured down on them. The car went headlong into them, crashing and splintering and throwing Fenny forward so she was pinned against the steering rod which struck into her body with the force of a hammer blow. There was a blurring of her vision, a spinning disc of light cutting objects in two. She felt a swimming in her head and a sudden shock of pain right inside her. She lay there conscious for about half a minute, and then was plunged into a darkness that was totally engulfing.

Shards of broken glass glintered in the sunlight and petrol seeped from the engine as the horn of the wrecked car broke the silence of the hills with its distress signal. A rough-coated dog sniffed around the trickles of oil, and suddenly a boy came running down the goat track with alarm and fear in his great dark eyes.

He looked inside the car, saw the girl pinned against the wheel, and smelled the strong odour of petrol. He wrenched desperately at the door, falling backwards into the dust as it suddenly came open. His strong young arms grabbed at Fenny's unconscious figure and he pulled her with fierce determination from the battered vehicle, dragging her along the road until they were out of range of that boiling engine which burst with a sudden roar, shooting flames and burning oil at the cliffside, and rolling in a tide of smoke and fire over the body of the car.

Fenny lay on the road in her torn and dirty dress, and she knew nothing of her rescue. The car burned noisily, and the goat-dog crouched by the boy as he watched over her, waiting for the smoke and flames to bring help from the village.

CHAPTER SEVEN

THE glimmering lamp light played over the dark masculine features, and as in a mist Fenny saw the irregular pulsing of a vein in the brown neck, where the dark shirt lay open. A slither of the light was caught and held in the golden disc on a chain, and she frowned slightly and was aware of something not quite right. Her eyes stole over the lean face and as the weary mistiness cleared from her gaze, that aching weight settled on her heart again.

'Hi there,' Zonar smiled, and took her hands into his, carrying them gently to his lips. 'You know me, eh? Now you recognize me?'

She nodded and had a feeling that she had thought him someone else, and that she had spoken the name of that other person.

'It's good to see you back with us.' He spoke softly, warmly, and continued to hold her fine-boned hands in his strong ones. 'Glad to be back, Fenella?'

'I feel – as if I'd been a long way away.' Her eyes stole around the room and the familiarity of the place began to creep back to her as she gazed at the icon in its niche softly glowing, the tiny golden hands of the Virgin clasped together.

'What happened, Zonar?' Her eyes dwelt again upon his face, and now there was no mistaking the good-looking features, the more youthful set to them despite the rakish lines beside the dark eyes.

'You were in a skirmish with the cliffs when a dog ran in front of the car you were driving. A boy from the village dragged you free of the wreckage before it burst into flames. He's quite the young hero.'

'I'm glad a – and grateful to him.' Yes, there in her

aching heart was the memory of that moment when the car had gone out of control and had slammed into the fire-coloured cliffs; a shudder ran through her and Zonar's hands tightened on hers.

'Don't think any more about it,' he said. 'It's over with and you are safe with us, and on the mend.'

'What am I mending from?' Her eyes wouldn't leave his, searching for what lay behind his words. 'How long have I been – ill?'

'Several days,' he told her. 'Mostly you have slept and have drowsily rallied so the nurse could feed you with chicken broth.'

'Several – days,' she repeated. 'I – I don't remember them at all, so I must have been out of my mind. Was I hit on the head, Zonar?'

'Yes, when the car crashed. The cut is under your hair, so there won't be a scar.'

'Scars,' she murmured. 'Yes, I have those.'

'No,' he shook his head, leaning forward and looking intently into her eyes. 'Your face wasn't touched, my dear.'

My dear. How those two words brought a rush of memories, both bitter and sweet ... other, more workworn hands holding hers, and lips that came down on hers and crushed to a whimper all that clamoured in her heart for utterance.

'I don't care about my face,' she said, and remorseless and sudden came the truth, flooding through her in a long silent scream. 'I – I've lost my baby, haven't I?'

That pulse in Zonar's throat seemed to kick against his skin, and his dark lashes came half-down over his dark eyes. 'I – I'm afraid so, Fenella. We knew you would have to be told and the doctor thought I should be the one to tell you – in place of Lion.'

'I see.' She said it in a toneless voice and there were no

tears in her to be shed. Perhaps she had wept them unaware, but right now her eyes were dry and her body was empty. 'Is he too angry with me to – to come and see me?'

'My dear girl, we can't locate him! He has gone off in the *Cyrene* and we've been trying for days to get in touch with him. We have tried all his old haunts—'

'Have you tried his old girl-friends?' she asked cynically. 'Have you thought of cabling to New York, where my cousin is?'

Zonar stared down at her and an expression of shock came into his eyes. 'You can't believe that? Lion wouldn't—'

'Lion loves her, and he and I parted on bitter terms. Now – now he has something else to add to his list against me. I'm the wife he never wanted, and now I have killed his child. Could I do more to make him hate the very thought of me?'

'Ah, Fenella, what can I say to console you?' Zonar gripped her hands and had that look of a strong man confronted by a pain he was helpless to alleviate, that of a woman who has tormentedly lost something that was part of her very heart. 'But none of us knew except old Kassandra, and it was she who pulled you through while we waited for the doctor to come. She kept muttering something about there being only one chance – did she mean that the child was your one chance of making your marriage work?'

Fenella thought of what Kassandra had predicted – that she would have only one child, and now that child was no more.

'Did Lion know about the baby?' Zonar asked. 'Had you told him?'

She shook her head against the pillow, her hair braided for coolness in a single thick plait against her nightdress.

160

The definition of Fenny's cheekbones was more pronounced, with shadows beneath them, and her arms looked thin against the silk coverlet of the bed. She looked young and hurt and lost... now there was nothing for her to hold of her strange marriage. It had broken into pieces and there was no mending what had never been a perfect thing.

If only... oh God, if only this aching need of Lion had died with his child, but still it was there, gnawing at her heart like a live thing... all she had to take away with her from Petaloudes

'Perhaps if you had told him, Fenella, he might not have gone away.' Zonar's black brows drew together above the bridge of his finely shaped nose. 'I think Lion would have been overjoyed—'

'Oh yes,' she said, the cynicism in her eyes again. 'He only kept me with him so I could give him a child – that was the bargain he made with me. I would remain his wife until I became the mother of his son, and then it would all be over. I – I didn't want him to know that I was going to have his child of a cold, calculating passion. I wanted to pretend for a while that I had something secret and precious that was mine alone – I was going to run away with it! Does that shock you, brother-in-law? I was going away while Lion was off on his cruise, and I intended to hide away somewhere in England where he would never find me. One of our country villages, tucked away in the West Country. I had it all planned, and then the fates stepped in – in the shape of a half-wild goat-dog. Goats, symbols of Pan, the devil-god of pagan mythology. Here on a Greek island one begins to believe in the force of pagan things – do you believe in them, Zonar, or are you too much the man of the world?'

'I am foremost a Greek,' he said. 'I believe that the gods hand out gifts and make us pay for them.'

161

'I stole mine,' she said, 'so your gods punished me. It has been a cruel punishment – now I have nothing, and it even hurts too much for me to cry.'

'Fenella,' he brought her hands up against his face and pressed their coldness to his warm skin, 'dull people create no drama, they love and suffer in a tepid way. But you – you're a lovely, emotional, giving girl, and so you take to heart everything that happens to you. You took Lion to your heart – you can if you try throw him out of it!'

She felt beneath the tips of her fingers the hard shapely bones of Zonar's face; she saw in his eyes what he was asking of her. Oh, how easy to turn to him and take kindness in place of coldness ... he pressed her fingers down over his face to his throat, so warm and pulsing.

'We'll go away together,' he said softly. 'You have only to say the word, little one.'

'No!'

The word sprang from her heart itself. 'No ... I won't add brother stealing to my other crimes, Zonar. I won't be the cause of anguish and hatred between you and Lion. He brought you up – you and Metre. He cared for you, starved for you, worked in quarries and on ships so you could have a good life. Please, let go of my hands. Please stop saying these things ...'

'When you're stronger, Fenella. When everything has stopped hurting so much, then we'll talk again. We have our lives to live, and I want you for yourself. You! So sweet and fair and cool-skinned.'

He turned the palms of her hands to his lips and kissed them ... there where Kassandra had looked and seen shadows.

Fenella sighed and felt helpless to reason with Zonar right now, and it was a relief when the nurse came into the room, uniformed and briskly firm with Zonar.

'The *kyria* is still very fatigued,' she told him. 'In the

morning she will be feeling very much brighter.'

'Then *kali andamosi*.' He smiled down into Fenny's eyes, then rose to his feet and sauntered to the door, where he gave the nurse a bow and a quizzical look. When the door closed behind him, the nurse smoothed Fenny's pillows and gave her a drink of lime juice.

'It is nice of a husband's brother to be so concerned,' she said. 'A kind young man – he had tears in his eyes when he was told of your miscarriage. Greek men take these things to heart.'

Fenny looked pensively at the nurse. 'Will I – will there ever be the possibility of another child?' she asked.

'You must ask the doctor, *kyria*.' The woman turned away, looking rather evasive as she tidied the things on the bedside table.

'Please, can't you tell me? You're a midwife and I feel sure that you know – and I shan't burst into tears, I promise.'

'Why?' The nurse turned again to look at Fenny. 'Are you another of these modern young women who don't really care to have a family?'

'I – I care very much, but I don't like to be left in the dark about something so – so important to me.' Fenny reached out and caught at the starched cuff. 'You know, don't you?'

'These things are never certain, *kyria*. In a few years—'

'Years?' Fenny breathed. 'I'm afraid I can't look that far ahead.'

'The young never can.' A smile moved across the woman's face, softening its severity. 'I will tell you this. There would have been some complications attending the birth, had you gone your full term. Giving birth might have cost you much.'

'My life?' Fenny felt as if she had been punched over

the heart. Oh God, she would have died and that baby would have been put into a home, had she run away from Lion. 'Is that what you're saying, nurse?'

'I shouldn't tell you, but in these matters we get to know, though the doctors don't like to think that our knowledge is so good. Yes, you might well have died.'

Fenny absorbed this, and then asked quietly: 'Was it possible to tell if the child would have been a boy?'

'It was a son, *kyria*.'

'I see.' Fenny closed her eyes in pain ... the son she would have borne Lion, to grow up in his image and to have, perhaps, a little of her in him. The son Lion might never have known, and now would never know.

He would only know about all this when he returned from his trip, having gone sailing off on the *caique* without even telling his brothers where he could be located in the event of an emergency. Even business, for once, seemed of less importance to him than this sudden need to get away from everybody.

Everybody? Fenny had cynically told Zonar to make contact with New York, where Penela was working in the theatre ... would it be so very strange if Lion were there? If he wanted Penela with every hardened sinew of him, then he wouldn't let an unwanted wife stand in his way, and as Fenella knew, it had always been exciting to her cousin to have a married man in pursuit of her.

'You mustn't grieve too much or you won't get well.' The nurse touched a cool, well-scrubbed hand to Fenny's forehead. 'It will be better for your husband when he comes home to find you recovered and not looking wan and sick. The sad things that happen to us have to be borne as bravely as possible, and he has you—'

'Me?' Fenny gave a laugh that was as hollow as her heart felt. 'He'll never forgive me when he finds out what has happened. He'll blame me for everything.'

'Very naturally he will be disappointed, *kyria*, but he will understand that the accident was not your fault. We aren't to blame for what is already marked out for us; each pleasure has its price, and each pain its panacea.'

'I only wish I could believe you, nurse, but my heart feels empty, and my pain too acute for any remedy to ease it – short of joining my poor little baby.'

'You must try not to be morbid, *kyria*. If you had been meant to die with the child, then you would have done so.'

'You believe in fate, I see?' That cynical smile crept into Fenny's eyes. 'It was rather unkind of fate to take away from me the only child I was meant to have, and to have even made it almost certain that I'd die having my son. He came to me in love – my love for the man who gave him to me.'

Fenny turned her face into her pillows with these words and her throat ached with the love and loss that she felt and couldn't relieve with her frozen tears.

'Go to sleep,' the nurse murmured. 'Tomorrow things will look much brighter for you, and when your full strength returns you will wonder that you ever wanted to die. *Kalinikta, kyria.*'

'Goodnight, nurse. Thank you for being kind.'

The bedside lamp was extinguished and a moment later the bedroom door closed quietly behind the uniformed figure. Only the glow of the *lampada* lit the room, only the ticking of the clock broke the silence, only the bitter remained to Fenny of having lain in Lion's arms and known a fleeting joy.

A joy she had stolen from behind the wedding veil of another girl, and here on this pagan Greek isle the gods had punished her for daring to fly in their faces.

She drifted on the edge of sleep as beyond the softly blowing curtains the sea washed over the rocks strewn at the foot of the cliffs ... the fire-coloured cliffs on which the *kastello* was built, its foundations carved from the stone itself so that it stood in sure and dominant strength. It was only the people inside the house that seemed so vulnerable, so capable of being hurt, and Fenny stirred restlessly in her bed and felt as if this Greek house had a blight on it.

A house where love was not made welcome ... it had rejected Zonar's young wife, and now Lion's son was only a stab of agony and a cold little memory.

'Oh, Lion!' Fenny flung her arms across the pillows and hugged them in her loneliness, and her fear of the future. 'Come away with me,' Zonar had said to her. 'I care about you – you!'

It was only when Fenny was much stronger and able to sit on her *moussandra* in the sunlight that they told her a little plaque to the baby's memory had been erected at the chapel in the hills. 'I'd like to see it,' she told Adelina, and on the first day she was allowed out of the house, Zonar and Adelina took her by car to the chapel and she walked with them among the cypress trees to the quiet corner where the little bronze plaque had been placed. On it were inscribed just a few words in Greek and the name Heraklion Mavrakis Junior.

Still tearless, still unable to cry, Fenny laid freesias on the tiny grave and stroked her fingers across the Greek lettering. 'What do the words say?' she asked.

'He plucked the flower of life,' Zonar told her, bending to raise her to her feet.

'But he never did, poor little boy. There was never a chance for him – he was just a curled-up, tiny embryo, struck dead by the steering rod of a car. I'd like to scream for him, tear my hair, and curse the gods of your island.'

'My dear,' said Adelina, 'do look on the sunny side. You could be lying there with that scrap of life. Hold out your hand and feel the sun on your skin, and look how attractive you are in that smoke-grey chiffon of mine. How fortunate I had the dress and it fitted you. Does she not look fetching, Zonar?'

Adelina cast a knowing look at her brother-in-law, who was staring at Fenny's hair in the sunlight falling down through the green spires of the trees and making it shine against the delicate shape of her face.

'Yes,' he said, and his hard white teeth bit down on his lip as if he forcibly repressed what he shouldn't be feeling for his brother's wife. 'I know how you feel, Fenella, but believe me, the aching and the anger go away in time; they fade into the far corners of the heart and life becomes worth living again.'

'Of course it does.' Adelina tucked an arm through Fenny's. 'You must learn to have some fun, my dear. Zonar is taking us across to Athens in a a day or so, and between us we'll shake you out of the blues. You will come, won't you, pet? Lion is playing the absent landlord, so you don't have to ask his permission – he should have let us know where we could reach him, but instead he went prowling off like a sulky lion with a thorn in his side. Men! They are the root cause of most of our sufferings!'

'My dear sister-in-law,' Zonar smiled crookedly, 'when have you ever suffered? Metre is the soul of patience with you, having been cut from less complicated cloth than Lion and myself. You should count your blessings.'

'I made sure, Zonar, that the man I married wasn't subtle and deep, with ground glass mixed into his personality. Did you know that my father even considered Lion for my potential husband, but despite your older brother's brain and zest I soon let it be known to Papa that I would sooner walk into a lion's den than be married to Heraklion Mavrakis. I would say that poor Fenella has learned her lesson.'

Fenny heard what Adelina said, but she merely gave a slight, non-committal smile. She had to learn to hide her bruised feelings and the sooner the better. They walked away from the little bronze plaque and she felt as if she left some of her heart behind her in the ground. Zonar took her hand and tucked it into the crook of his arm and for a brief moment his fingers pressed hers. He understood as Adelina never could, for like her he had married for love.

They walked through the gardens of the chapel, where old stone tombs stood in the sunlight, with their carved weepers, hooded and cloaked. Fenny glanced at them and felt as if she, too, wept tears of stone.

As they drove home the quail were flying over the clumps of herbs on the hillsides and the air was richly scented with thyme and pine-sap. They passed the cliffs where she had crashed and she saw the black burn marks where the grass had been sheared off in the heat and the scorch scars against the cliff-face.

'I hope the goat-boy was rewarded,' she said. 'He was brave to drag me from the car.'

'His dog caused the damage, darling,' said Adelina. 'He admitted that when some men of the village brought you home to us in a farm cart. When you come to think of it, Zonar, this is a very primitive island. It should have its own hospital.'

'Lion is considering it,' Zonar told her. 'No doubt when he learns of Fenella's accident he will go ahead with his plans to build one.'

'What did you do for the boy?' Fenny asked her brother-in-law. 'I feel in his debt, you know. He could have been hurt himself.'

'I have talked with the lad's father and let him know that Lion will want to reward him, probably with a gift of money or a herd of goats of his own. Livestock is precious to these people. It's more than money in the bank as far as they're concerned. They have, you see, a way of life that Lion is afraid of spoiling, and that is the reason he goes slowly in the matter of modernizing the island. He has seen it done elsewhere, and before you can look round the tourists are there and tinpot hotels are going up right on the beaches, spoiling the beauty and the people. But a hospital is a necessity, and Lion has talked of this. He cares about people, whether you believe it or not, Adelina.'

'I think he cares about his own image,' Adelina rejoined. 'King of his own particular jungle – you must forgive me, Zonar, if I find your brother a hard man.'

'His life has never been gentle.' Zonar shrugged his shoulders. 'Our early years mark us. Deprivations and struggles can't help but harden the muscles of the body and the emotions. He takes some understanding, I will admit that.'

'Understanding is a mild word.' Adelina gave a look at Fenny. 'It wouldn't please me to have a husband go off in his *caique* without a word of where he was going. It isn't like him, though. He usually has business on his mind to the exclusion of everything else. What is up with the man?'

'I think he wanted to get away from me,' Fenny said quietly. 'He and I had a – a difference of opinion before he left. I – I'm not looking forward to his return—'

'Then we'll go to Athens for a few days.' Adelina smiled at the prospect. 'You will take us, Zonar?'

'With pleasure.' His voice came warm and deep to Fenny's ears. 'I think a short holiday will be immensely good for Fenella. She will enjoy the distractions of Athens – the shops, the sights, and the music. Leave all the arrangements to me, ladies. I shall ensure that we have a good time.'

'One thing I'll say for you, Zonar,' Adelina reached her slim hand to him and stroked her tinted fingernails down his lean cheek, 'you are not only handsome, you are very human. Fenella should have married you, dear boy.'

'I expected her to be a bridesmaid at my brother's wedding,' he drawled, 'and I made my plans accordingly.'

As he brought the car to a halt in the courtyard of the *kastello* he cast a quizzical look at Fenella. 'Dare I make a few more plans?' he asked. 'Or will you again surprise me?'

'I – I just don't want to get involved in any more love tangles.' Her smile was pensive. 'I'm heart-empty, and I just want to learn how to take life less seriously. I want to learn from you two how to keep my head out of the clouds and my heart under control, so let my lessons start from today, please. Don't let us talk of anything but the fun we'll have together.'

'Be my pupil, dear, and you will pass your lessons with flying colours,' Adelina laughed. 'Life can be a pleasure if you don't take it to heart.'

But as Adelina spoke, Zonar was looking at Fenella, and his hands as they rested on the wheel of the silent car were showing their white knuckles under the sun-tanned skin.

Fenny was aware that Zonar was studying her, but she refused to meet his eyes. She had to learn how to be proof against the hurts of love, and she wasn't going to let this lean charmer patch up her broken life . . . not yet.

They went indoors and Adelina ordered tea to be served on the terrace overlooking the lemon groves, where some of the workers were singing as they tended to the fruit trees. A Greek song with its strange half-sad cadences, drifting back and forth, a mysterious tide of melody. Fenny leaned back in her cane chair and gave herself up to the moment; the sun on her face, and the congenial presence of Zonar Mavrakis. He gave her what Lion had never given – his unstinting belief in her as a selfless person.

But from now on she would no longer be selfless and wide-open to pain. Now she would search for a sensuous pleasure in the good things of life ... taking instead of giving, like Penela and Adelina.

A delicious brew of tea was served to them, along with honey puffs and custard tarts. They sat there talking idly for about an hour, until the sun began to slide down towards the sea. They watched the sunset as it flamed with a glorious fire, as if to express all that was pagan and untamed in this land of the sun-god. Then came the fading gold and flame, the deepening shadows in the groves, and beyond them the sea rolling in gilded scrolls above which the seabirds cried.

Adelina went off to her husband, and Fenny could just catch the glint of Zonar's eyes as he slipped a cheroot between his lips and fired the tip. Into his pocket slid his case and back went his head as he savoured a deep lungful of smoke.

'That was a splendid sunset,' he murmured. 'Your eyes were glowing as you watched it.'

'I never cease to wonder at Greek splendours,' she half-smiled. 'All things here have a touch of the pagan, haven't they?'

'The wine and the tears,' he said. 'The enjoyment and the endurance. Tell me, will you remain in Greece?'

The unexpected question took her breath away for a moment – so he had guessed that she was planning to go away after this trip to Athens. He knew that everything was over between her and his brother; that there could be no sort of reconciliation.

'I must go away,' she said. 'You do understand, don't

you?'

'Of course. There has to be love in a marriage or there is nothing. You know, despite the way Adelina talks of her marriage, there is something enduring between her and Metre. They suit each other.'

'That is the way it should be – to suit each other.' The wind off the sea combed Fenny's hair from her brow, and everything was cool and dusky now the sun had died away. And way up there in the sky a slim shell of a moon was taking shape, a misty ghost as yet among the stars.

'I think you have grown to love Greece, and there are other islands.' The smoke of the cheroot drifted to her, but it couldn't plague her, for Zonar used a milder blend of tobacco from his brother. 'Are you afraid of Lion – to live with him, and to run away from him? How far will you run, Fenella? To the ends of your heart?'

'I can't stay with a man who doesn't want me,' she said. 'We don't suit, he and I. We have only conflict and no contentment. I find it in me to envy Adelina, for she has what suits her, as you said.'

'They call it need,' Zonar told her. 'We all need someone, to a high-voltage degree or a low one. I'd like to give you time to need me, and I believe you could. You aren't meant to be alone, certainly not in the future, having lived as you have with a man, and having carried his child inside you.'

'I can have no more children, Zonar.' She gave him a tortured smile. 'I have become half a woman.'

'Never that!' He said it with a soft vehemence. 'You are what you are, not just a body for the breeding of a son. I have a son. Let me make you the mother of my Aleko—'

And there he broke off as someone came through the glass doors on to the terrace, a slight rustle of starch in the skirt of her nursemaid's uniform.

'I hope you don't mind me reminding you, sir, but it is time for you to play with Aleko before I give him his bath and his supper.'

The voice was polite enough, but Fenny felt sure that the young woman had heard what Zonar had said about his son. A little knot of nerves seemed to tighten in her midriff, for she was still Lion's wife and the last thing she wanted was to leave Petaloudes with people thinking that Zonar had broken up his brother's marriage.

He rose lazily to his feet. 'Come with me,' he said to Fenny. 'The boy will enjoy a game with the two of us, and I'd like him to get to know you better.'

She almost said she would come to the nursery, and then she heard that rustle of starch again and felt the look which the nursemaid flung at her in the half-light of the terrace. 'I'm a little weary,' she said. 'I'll just sit here a while longer and enjoy my solitude.'

'If that is what you want.' He leaned down to her and – in front of that girl – lightly touched her cheek. 'Dream about Athens and the good times we shall have there. See you later.'

He went away with his son's nurse, and Fenny was left alone with the pensive feeling that she and Zonar were drifting, almost inevitably, into a dangerous intimacy. They were both lonely ... they had both lost someone who had meant a lot to them.

She gazed up at the moon as it slowly filled with gold, a slipper of a lamp that cast a cool, serene glow over the terrace. From the shadowed garden came the rustling of vines and the purring of cicadas, and it was all so calm and so in contrast to her inner feelings. It was a kind of melancholy that she felt; an acceptance of things as they were. She was touched by the beauty of the night, but in a distant way, as if never again would she thrill to the magic. Far out on the sea she could make out the night lanterns of the fishing boats; the lights were said to attract the fish who came swimming up into the nets like so many moths to the flame.

There was beauty to life, but there was cruelty as well, and Fenny swore to herself that never again would she let her heart lead her into the flame that held ecstasy and ashes.

She rose and left the terrace and made her way to her apartment in the tower. When she arrived on the gallery she found Kassandra there, lurking about in the shadows. The woman greeted her quietly, and then followed her into the sitting-room of the suite. 'The *kyria* is looking much better,' she said. 'But I have been sad for you, and I have heard you call out for your man and not have him come to you.'

'I shall never call out again, Kassandra, and I don't plan to remain here.' Fenny tinkered with an ornament, and then met the older woman's eyes in a wall mirror. 'It had to be – you know that, don't you? You saw it in my hand that first night I came here. Then I was a stranger to Greece and I didn't believe in such things, but I shall never be sceptical again. I have learned how dangerous it is to dare the gods.'

'Will the *kyria* let me read her palm again?' Kassandra asked.

'No!' Fenny thrust her hands behind her. 'I know the future for myself and I – I just couldn't bear to have it verified. Let it rest, please. Let me learn how to forget.'

'As the *kyria* wishes.' Kassandra gazed steadily at Fenny with her strange eyes. 'Danger, love, loyalty, these are the fires of the spirit, you know. They make us and they break us, and we must have the courage to face up to them.'

'I think my courage has run out of me,' Fenny said. 'I can't take any more—'

'And you are going away, *kyria*?'

'Yes – soon.'

'With the brother of the *kyrios*?'

'Yes.'

'Then God help you!'

Kassandra turned and left the room, closing the door with a sharp click that played on Fenny's nerves. Oh God, did these people think she was made of stone to take any more? She wasn't Greek. She hadn't been bred to their kind of endurance, for her idea of marriage was warmth, protection, and a firm shoulder to find strength on. She had none of these, and couldn't face a future without them.

She sank on nerveless legs to the carpet and buried her face against the divan cushions, gripping them with her fingers until she felt as if her bones were breaking through her skin. She couldn't face Lion, and she wanted to be gone from the *kastello* before he returned. She had paid dearly for ever marrying him in the guise of her cousin; he couldn't have hoped for a sweeter, more bitter revenge than to have helped to cut out her heart.

They made a definite arrangement to go across to the mainland and Zonar booked rooms for them at the Achilles Hotel in the heart of Athens, with views of the Acropolis from its windows.

And then came a change of plan for Adelina when she received word that her father wasn't very well and wished to see her. Being the only daughter, Adelina was instantly concerned and she packed a bag and went off in the launch which had been sent to collect her, waving dramatically to her husband as he stood there on the beach, looking rather lost.

'Poor Lina,' he said, shaking his head. 'She is desperately fond of her *patir,* and added to it she has to lose this trip to Athens. She was so looking forward to a shopping spree.'

Demetre glanced at his brother. 'You will postpone it, eh? With no chaperone for Fenella you will wait until my Lina returns from seeing her father?'

He spoke Fenny's name rather stiffly, still obstinate about accepting her – maybe because Zonar his twin so obviously liked her.

'No, there's no need to put off the trip, for Adelina can join us later on.' Zonar looked directly at Fenny. 'You are looking forward to seeing Athens, aren't you?'

'Very much.' She spoke with a touch of defiance. 'Unless you feel that we should wait until Adelina can travel with us?'

'I see no real reason for waiting. You need a holiday to help you recover fully from your – accident. It's a pity about Adelina, but there you are. Her father comes first.'

'I think you should put it off,' his brother said sharply. 'Be reasonable, Zonar. Fenella is not your wife! She belongs to Lion!'

'But I don't!' The words flashed through Fenny's mind, though she didn't actually speak them aloud. 'I've never belonged to him in the truest sense of the word – Metre had it right in the first place, when he called me an intruder.'

'Zonar's right,' she said, looking at Demetre. 'I need very much to get away from the island and the memories it holds for me. I want to go to Athens more than anything, and I can always go alone if you feel that propriety will be offended if I go with Zonar.'

Demetre drew his black brows together until they almost met in a scowl. 'Lion has his good name to consider and it isn't right for a wife to run around with another man. Haven't you been enough of a trial to

176

Lion?'

'Oh yes, I'm aware that I've been a trial to him, Metre, but out of sight, out of mind. I'm going to Athens whether I go alone or not.'

'There is no question of you going alone, Fenella.' Zonar spoke firmly. 'We are both adults, and to the devil with propriety. We go as arranged – tomorrow.'

'Lion won't like this,' Demetre warned. 'You know what a temper he has, Zonar, when something really arouses it. It's Fenella's place as his wife to be here and to acquaint him with the facts of her accident.'

'Really, brother?' Zonar's lean face was suddenly dark with anger. 'Was he here when she was racked head and foot with the agony of losing his child? Was he by her side to offer his comfort and his caring? It was for me to do that, and it's for me to take her where the bright lights are and the music. It's for me to put back the lights in her eyes, and I couldn't care a devil what you or anyone else has to say in the matter. Next time Lion can lose his temper on me, not on this girl who has loved him. Look at her, Metre! She is only a slim and vulnerable girl like your Adelina, and she only asks to be protected – not to be lashed by an angry tongue because she cared about Lion's good name.'

Zonar breathed deeply and thrust a black strand of hair from his blazing eyes. 'To hell with Lion's good name! To hell with him! Let us hope he's with that showy, artificial blonde he prefers to a real woman!'

'Please,' Fenny clutched at Zonar's arm, feeling the tense muscles under her grip, 'don't quarrel with Metre over me. He's concerned for Adelina, and he doesn't care about me. Quieten down, there's a good boy, and don't say things you'll regret. Some things that we say can never be unsaid, so don't talk about hell so easily. Hell is no pleasant place to be – I know!'

With dark eyes Zonar stared down at Fenny, then the muscles of his face slowly relaxed and a brief smile touched his lips. 'Why do we worry about other people?' he asked.

'Because we aren't completely selfish.'

'But we still go to Athens – together?'

'Yes.' She spoke with a touch of fatalism. 'I'm letting happen what has to happen – my face naked, Zonar, not veiled.'

'You two,' Demetre exclaimed, 'you are going to make unhappiness for yourselves, and for others. Can't you see that?'

'I refuse to see beyond tomorrow.' Zonar stood there staring towards the sea, on that shore where the rocks were mantled in seaweed that curled and gleamed like living jade in the sunlight. 'You won't understand, brother, because passion is not your cross. You have what suits you, but Fenella and I have to go in search of our star. It may shine like a jewel in our sky, or it may fall and burn out – there in the sea. At this very moment we can't tell, we can only follow it.'

As they walked back to the *kastello*, Fenny gazed up at the rambling white house, with its different levels of red-tiled roofs, and its tower like a Turkish minaret. There in that tower she had been a captive of her love for Lion; his prisoner of a bargain which was now ended. If one was fated to be hurt there seemed no way of avoiding it, and as they went indoors the sky overhead was a wild apricot and the surf seemed to throw a flamy glow upon the sands below them.

They flew across to Athens in the Alouette and booked into the Achilles Hotel, parting at the doors of their separate rooms with the conspiratorial smiles of two people on the threshold of a discovery. Fenny suspected that neither of them were sure of what it would bring, but for now they were eager – like two children who had run away from a stern guardian.

For the next few, light-hearted days they wandered around Athens and Fenny was shown the kind of places that only a real Greek would know about. Zonar took her off the tourist route to out-of-the-way *kafeneions*, into fascinating little shops that were like holes in the sun-scoured walls, with jutting balconies above filled to the brim with pots of basil and hanging geranium. They entered the old Turkish quarter where the market-place was still as it had been in the old days, with its coppersmiths, tapestry works, shoemakers and silk-weavers. There they bargained for a length of amber silk, with an old Turk in a skull-cup, with a long moustache and worry-beads slicking in his dark fingers. In the end he showed his teeth in a smile and spoke in Turkish to Zonar, and a minute later Fenny found herself in possession of the lovely silk.

'What did he say?' she asked, when they left that cave of glimmering colours, the package in her own straw bag, for Greek men never carried parcels.

Zonar glanced down at her and his own teeth showed in a smile. 'That the silk matched your hair, and that it would make a sleeping garment fit for a *houri*. He saw the rings on your hand and took me for your husband.'

Fenny glanced at her hand and surprise struck at her that not once had it occurred to her to remove the rings. Now was the time ... now was the moment, but it sped away and she knew deep down in her heart that she would only discard Lion's rings when her memory and her body had quite emptied of him.

They walked in the bronze evening sun of Greece, and they climbed to the flat-topped mount of the Acropolis, the highest point of the city, where they stood beneath the towering columns of the temple dedicated to the virgin goddess, Athena.

Lion's brother stood there in the sunlight like a lean, slightly weathered Greek god, and Fenny saw the female tourists look at him, and she saw in their eyes the wish that he was their companion instead of their own tubby, perspiring, unromantic-looking escorts. There was no denying the fact that Greek men had a touch of savage splendour about them, and as she smiled at the thought, Zonar caught her by the hand and ran her down the wide steps to where an old woman was selling pistachio nuts and raisins from a basket on her arm.

His eyes ran over her as they dawdled along eating nuts; she wore a charmingly simple apple-green dress and looked as if she might float off in the sunshine. 'The Greek sun loses itself in your hair,' he told her. 'Your skin is now a soft honey, and the shadows have retreated from your eyes. I wish I could say to the world that you are mine. People look at us and think it, but is it yet true, Fenella?'

'I – I don't know,' she replied. 'Isn't this enough for now?'

'Do you want it to be enough – for now?'

'Please,' she said. 'These carefree days with you, Zonar, have helped me so much. I'm so grateful to you.'

'Gratitude?' His smile was quizzical. 'I never thought the day would come when I'd thrill a little to that prosaic word! If you aren't careful, little one, you will be making a good fellow of me.'

'You're that already,' she smiled.

'Yes, I think I must be,' he drawled. 'This is the first time I've taken a girl on a platonic holiday.'

'But you're enjoying it, aren't you? It must make a change for you.'

He burst out laughing. 'Come along, Anglika, you give me several appetites, and one of them I can satisfy at the

Leaping Dolphin.'

This was a *taverna* in a garden of palm trees and almonds and clumps of scarlet oleander, where they had sizzling lamb straight off the spit, and vegetables in the rich gravy. As they ate and talked, some Greek workmen danced the *syrtakia,* their hands on each other's shoulders, having risen spontaneously from their seats as if driven to move and express their rough joy in life.

'This would never happen in England, eh?' Zonar leaned back with his glass of wine, and Fenny could feel his sandalled foot tapping beneath the table. 'A group of your sedate clerks rising in their lunch hour to perform one of your folk dances.'

She smiled at the image and shook her head. 'We're too shy,' she told him. 'Too self-conscious, and sad to say, some of the men are too tubby.'

'Are you shy of me?' he asked.

'No, not really.' And even as she said it, she recalled how acutely shy she had been of Lion — a mere glance from those lion eyes had been enough to make her feel as if she were blushing all over. 'I'm easy with you, Zonar, in the nicest sense of the word. I trust you more than anyone I've ever met — tell me, do you miss your little boy?'

'A bit,' he admitted. 'He's a quaint little thing, isn't he? He has his mother's eyes — she was a sweet creature, you know, and far too good for me. I — I didn't always give her reason to trust me, Fenella. Unlike Lion and Metre I was born with a roving eye. My two brothers are what you call single-hearted. They take to one woman and keep to her.'

Fenny lowered her gaze to the wine glass with which she tinkered. She thought of Penela, and wished to heaven her cousin had been worthy of Lion's devotion and single-hearted need of her. Life would have gone on for Fenny as it always had ... she would not have known

181

the trauma of loving a man who didn't love her ... she wouldn't have suffered the heartache of losing his baby.

'We shall go dancing tonight,' Zonar announced. 'Each Friday night, I am told, the hotel has a costume dance, with dominoes. Yes, this afternoon we'll go to a costumier's and rent a pair of fantastic garments. Are you game?'

'Oh yes, it will be great fun. I've never worn a mask—' And there she broke off and remembered the antique veil at the wedding, hiding her real face from Lion ... that virginal yashmak, as he had called it.

'Don't think about that!' Zonar had reached across and was gripping her hand. 'We all follow an impulse once in our lifetime, and you can't go on being punished for it. I won't let you! Come, drink your wine and finish your sweet, and we'll go looking for our disguises.'

That evening the hotel ballroom was adorned with balloons and fairy lights, and there was both a dance orchestra and several *bouzoukia* musicians, who in between the modern dancing played the compulsive, sensuously alive music of Greece. There was a mingling of brightly coloured costumes, and the black and gold dominoes made the eyes of the dancers look bold or mysterious, according to the sex of the wearer.

Fenny's costume was most attractive and made up of a small beaded cap, a bolero of velvet, a silk blouse with full embroidered sleeves, and a full velvet skirt over petticoats. Zonar was clad in black pantaloons, a ruffled silk shirt, and a stocking cap with a pom-pom on the end. He looked a cross between a pirate and a pierrot, and Fenny was laughing in his arms, a girl who had found a little forgetfulness for a while, when a hand clapped Zonar on the shoulder.

'I am cutting in, *kyrie*,' said an unforgettable voice, 'if you don't mind?'

Fenny stared into the man's eyes ... lion-gold eyes through the slits of the black mask. Though he was masked, the rest of him was clad soberly in a dark dress-suit and plain white shirt, black studs at the cuff of the hand he laid firmly on her partner's shoulder.

She felt Zonar go as taut as a length of steel, and then without a word he released her into his brother's arms. Very briefly his eyes met Fenny's and all the laughter had gone from them, then he gave that quizzical and gallant bow of his and walked off the floor.

The well-remembered arms tightened about Fenny, and looking into her husband's eyes she felt as if her knees were going to give way beneath her.

'I – I can't dance,' she said faintly. 'Please – take me outside.'

He did so, his arm locked with firm strength about her waist. Out there on the terrace she clutched at the cold stone of the balustrade and prayed that she wouldn't faint.

'Have I come as a shock?' he asked, and leaned his back against the stone and lifting a hand he took off his mask. The sun and the seawinds had darkened his skin to bronze, so that his eyes were brilliantly disturbing in his face.

'How did you find us!' A little of her strength was seeping back, but her traitorous heart that wouldn't listen to her mind was beating wildly in her breast. How fit he looked. How tall and hard. A lion into whose cage she had ventured, to be ripped and torn, and still her foolish heart had not learned its lesson.

'I was informed that you were here with Zonar – that you had come away with him.'

'Did Demetre tell you?'

'Metre is too attached to his twin to be disloyal and he

claimed not to know what was going on. I had to ask elsewhere, and I was told that you had come to Athens to have good times with my brother.'

'You spoke to Aleko's nurse, is that it? Or did she volunteer to unveil the scandalous details?'

'Are they scandalous?' He reached out and plucked the gold mask from Fenny's face, as if to see more clearly if she lied to him. 'Is Zonar your lover?'

'Lover?' she echoed, and now she was standing straight in front of him, and not clinging like a weak fool to the stonework. 'I have had only one lover in my life, Lion. Only one man who has known every inch of me without knowing a thing about me. A man with whom I made a baby ... a little thing I wanted very much, but which your ironic Greek gods took from me on the very day I went to the chapel to offer thanks that your arrogant head had not been blown off—'

'The child!' Suddenly Lion had hold of her with hands that were savage and yet strangely unhurting. 'You could have died and I would have been to blame—'

'No, the car ran off the road,' she broke in.

'I spoke with the doctor. He told me everything—'

'So now you know, Lion, that I have nothing left to give you. Nothing that you could possibly want. Your son is dead and I helped to kill him, though I would sooner have died myself. No doubt that's what you're thinking—'

'What I am thinking is that I have been a blind, high-handed brute to you!'

'Me?' She stared up at his face in the glow of the coloured lights and saw the bones carved and thrusting under the sun-darkened skin, with lines drawn hard down his lean cheeks.

'I have only this to say, Fenny, before you kick me out of your life – I loved you without knowing it, and when I came to know it, you no longer wanted me, and that is why I went off in the *Cyrene* like a sulky boy whose rare and pretty kite had flown off out of his rough hand.'

'You – loved me?' Her eyes filled with his dark face; her heart filled with wonder. 'But you despised me, Lion. You wanted Penela, and I believed you had gone off in search of her – that you could no longer stay away from her.'

'Penela?' He looked impatient. '*Melle mou*, I could no longer make out her face after a while with you. It was you who came in and out of my thoughts, sometimes in the very middle of a business conference. Your golden hair tumbling to your white shoulders, the large eyes soft as smoke, the hands like birds on my shoulders, like silk, then tipped with tiny swords that I felt for hours afterwards.

'God in heaven, I wanted to kill my own brother when that girl told me that you had left the island to be with him. Is it Zonar whom you love?'

'Of course I love him—'

'*Ah!*' It was a torn sound, ripping from Lion's throat, and his eyes seemed to go lifeless as they dwelt upon her in the play of the ruby, gold and sapphire lights.

'Zonar is the dearest, most understanding brother-in-law that a girl could ever hope to have.'

'Ah!' A different sound came into Lion's voice; a new sort of light began to burn in his eyes. All around them in the night was the sweet, heavy scent of flowers. 'Somehow I couldn't believe that you would run off and play those kind of games, but I had to find out for myself—'

'Why, Lion?' He had said he loved her, and if it were true – oh, so impossibly true, then she had to venture once again into his dangerous cage. 'Do you want a wife who can never give you a son?'

'I want *you*.' As he said it, the wonder of it was right

inside her. 'I never knew a woman who could be as generous as you, Fenny, as sweet and spirited and brave. My child would have killed you, do you hear? I want you alive and warm, slim and silky, giving and taking and filling up my heart. I wanted you with me on the *Cyrene*, but you said you didn't want to come. Nothing ever hurt me like that... by God, *nothing*.'

'It would have been heaven, but I thought you were going to send me away when our bargain about the baby—' She couldn't go on.

'I deserve to be flogged for making such a bargain with you. Ah, Fenny, can you really forgive me for being such a brute? In future I shall be reformed—'

'Yes, but not too much.' She let her arms steal around his neck, and when his hard body quivered against her, she tightened her arms and waited for his kiss.

He crushed her lips with his, warm and savage, the way she wanted them. The music played in the ballroom, and she hoped hazily that Zonar had found a pretty girl to dance with.

Masquerade
Historical Romances

Intrigue excitement romance...

Masquerade is an enthralling series of Historical Romances. As you read you will be transported back to an age of true romance . . . to the courts of eleventh-century Spain . . . to Regency England. From secret assignations in secluded country lanes to high intrigue in glittering chandelier-lit ballrooms.

You will lose yourself in a world where the smile of a beautiful woman could change the course of history.

Every month Masquerade offers you two new romances set against authentic historical backgrounds.

You'll find them where paperbacks are sold.

Just what the Doctor ordered!

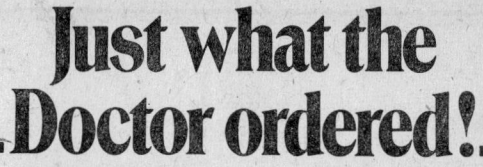

Don't miss the two Doctor-Nurse Romances published every month.

These titles highlight the romantic entanglements between doctors, nurses surgeons and sisters who are involved every day with life and death decisions. Surrounded as they are by constant pressure and emotion, it is no wonder that passions run high behind the scenes of modern hospital life.

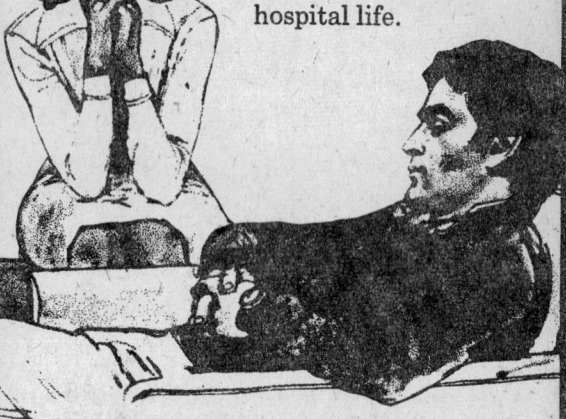

Available where you buy paperbacks. If you have difficulty in obtaining these at your normal retailer, contact Mills & Boon Reader Service, P.O. Box 236, Thornton Road, Croydon, CR9 3RU

Mills & Boon Best Seller Romances

~all that's best in romantic fiction

The best of Mills & Boon romances brought back for those who never had the opportunity of reading them on the first time of publication. Collect these stories of love and romance set in exotic, far-away places and fill your library with Mills & Boon Best Seller Romances.

Available where you buy paperbacks.

If you have difficulty in obtaining these at your normal retailer, contact Mills & Boon Reader Service, P.O. Box 236, Thornton Road, Croydon, CR9 3RU.

SAVE TIME, TROUBLE & MONEY!
By joining the exciting NEW...

Mills & Boon Romance CLUB

WITH all these EXCLUSIVE BENEFITS for every member

NOTHING TO PAY! MEMBERSHIP IS FREE TO REGULAR READERS!

IMAGINE the *pleasure* and *security* of having ALL your favourite *Mills & Boon* romantic fiction delivered right to *your* home, absolutely POST FREE... straight off the press! No waiting! No more disappointments! All this PLUS all the latest news of *new books* and *top-selling authors* in your own monthly MAGAZINE... PLUS *regular* big CASH SAVINGS... PLUS lots of wonderful strictly-limited, *members-only* SPECIAL OFFERS! All these exclusive benefits can be *yours* – right NOW – simply by joining the exciting NEW *Mills & Boon* ROMANCE CLUB. Complete and post the coupon below for FREE full-colour leaflet. It costs nothing. HURRY!

No obligation to join unless you wish!

FREE CLUB MAGAZINE Packed with *advance* news of latest titles and authors

Exciting offers of FREE BOOKS For club members ONLY

Lots of fabulous BARGAIN OFFERS –many at BIG CASH SAVINGS

FREE FULL-COLOUR LEAFLET!
CUT OUT *CUT-OUT COUPON BELOW AND POST IT TODAY!*

To: MILLS & BOON READER SERVICE, P.O. Box No 236, Thornton Road, Croydon, Surrey CR9 3RU, England.
WITHOUT OBLIGATION to join, please send me FREE details of the exciting NEW Mills & Boon ROMANCE CLUB and of all the exclusive benefits of membership.

Please write in BLOCK LETTERS below

NAME (Mrs/Miss) ....

ADDRESS ....

CITY/TOWN ....

COUNTY/COUNTRY .... POST/ZIP CODE ....

Readers in South Africa and Zimbabwe please write to:
P.O. BOX 1872, Johannesburg, 2000. S. Africa

CUT OUT AND POST THIS PAGE TO RECEIVE

FREE
FULL COLOUR Mills & Boon CATALOGUE

and – if you wish – why not also ORDER NOW any (or all) of the favourite titles offered overleaf?

Because you've enjoyed *this* Mills & Boon romance so very much, you'll really *love* choosing more of your favourite romantic reading from the fascinating, sparkling full-colour pages of "Happy Reading" – the *complete* Mills & Boon catalogue. It not only lists ALL our current top-selling love stories, but it also brings you *advance news* of all our exciting NEW TITLES *plus* lots of super SPECIAL OFFERS! And it comes to you complete with a convenient, easy-to-use DIRECT DELIVERY Order Form.

Imagine! No more *waiting*! No more "sorry – sold out" disappointments! HURRY! Send for *your* FREE Catalogue NOW . . . and ensure a REGULAR supply of all your best-loved Mills & Boon romances this happy, carefree, DIRECT DELIVERY way! But why wait?

Why not – *at the same time* – ORDER NOW a few of the highly recommended titles listed, for your convenience, *overleaf*? It's so simple! Just tick *your* selection(s) on the back and complete the coupon below. Then post *this whole page* – with your remittance (including correct postage and packing) for speedy *by-return* despatch.

✱POST TO: MILLS & BOON READER SERVICE, P.O. Box 236 Thornton Road, Croydon, Surrey CR9 3RU, England.

Please tick ☑ (as applicable) below:–

☐ Please send me the FREE Mills & Boon Catalogue

☐ As well as my FREE Catalogue please send me the title(s) I have ticked ☑ overleaf

I enclose £................ (No C.O.D.) Please add 25p postage and packing for one book. 15p postage and packing per book for two to nine books (maximum 9 x 15p = £1.35). For TEN books or more FREE postage and packing.

Please write in BLOCK LETTERS below

NAME (Mrs./Miss)...

ADDRESS ....

CITY/TOWN...

COUNTY/COUNTRY............................POSTAL/ZIP CODE..............

Readers in South Africa and Zimbabwe please write to: P.O. BOX 1872, Johannesburg, 2000. S. Africa

Choose from this selection of Mills & Boon FAVOURITES — ALL HIGHLY RECOMMENDED

ORDER NOW FOR DIRECT DELIVERY

- ☐ 1683 WHERE THE WOLF LEADS *Jane Arbor*
- ☐ 1684 THE DARK OASIS *Margaret Pargeter*
- ☐ 1685 BAREFOOT BRIDE *Dorothy Cork*
- ☐ 1686 A TOUCH OF THE DEVIL *Anne Weale*
- ☐ 1687 THE SILVER THAW *Betty Neels*
- ☐ 1688 THE DANGEROUS TIDE *Elizabeth Graham*
- ☐ 1689 MARRIAGE IN HASTE *Sue Peters*
- ☐ 1690 THE TENDER LEAVES *Essie Summers*
- ☐ 1691 LOVE AND NO MARRIAGE *Roberta Leigh*
- ☐ 1692 THE ICE MAIDEN *Sally Wentworth*
- ☐ 1693 NO PASSING FANCY *Kay Thorpe*
- ☐ 1694 HEART OF STONE *Janet Dailey*
- ☐ 1695 WHEN LIGHTNING STRIKES *Jane Donnelly*
- ☐ 1696 SHADOW OF DESIRE *Sara Craven*
- ☐ 1697 FEAR OF LOVE *Carole Mortimer*
- ☐ 1698 WIFE BY CONTRACT *Flora Kidd*
- ☐ 1699 WIFE FOR A YEAR *Roberta Leigh*
- ☐ 1700 THE WINDS OF WINTER *Sandra Field*
- ☐ 1701 FLAMINGO PARK *Margaret Way*
- ☐ 1702 SWEET NOT ALWAYS *Karen van der Zee*

ONLY 65p EACH

SIMPLY TICK √ YOUR SELECTION(S) ABOVE, THEN JUST COMPLETE AND POST THE ORDER FORM OVERLEAF